Broken Dreams

Dedication

To my dear mother, the late Mrs Patricia N.Adibe:
Mama, your loving memory remains evergreen and
we miss you everyday.

To my wife, Ngo:
What can I say to properly capture what you mean to
me? That you are the thread that holds everything
together in my life is an understatement.

To my children, Adaobi, Udoka and Nnedi:
My angels, without your unconditional love and
appreciation, things will certainly not be the same.

To brothers Emeka and Ifeanyi, and sisters Cecilia,
Kate, Anthonia and Georgina: Knowing that I can
always count on your absolute love and support is an
exceptional source of strength.

To Baffour Ankomah and Kayode Soyinka,
for the confidence you showed in me.

Broken Dreams

Jideofor Adibe

Published by
Adonis & Abbey Publishers Ltd
P.O. Box 43418
London
SE11 4XZ
www.adonis-abbey.com

First edition, June 2003

British Library Cataloguing-in-Publication Data
A catalogue record for this book is available from the British Library

ISBN 0-9545037-0-8

Editor: Steve Mackey
Cover design: Ifeanyi Adibe.

Printed and bound in Great Britain by Lightning Source UK

1

The tension outside was real. Even the most stubborn man could feel it in his veins. The entire animal kingdom also knew what was happening, had held many meetings about it and tried to communicate its displeasure and concerns to as many as cared to listen. There were, for instance, the owls that seemed to be everywhere, lamenting the impending apocalypse. Even Joe, the clever weaverbird that for two years solid had serenaded us from dawn to dusk, had withdrawn her labour. It was the first time she had been absent from duty in two years, and the import of her absence added a mystical, ghostly quality to the almost tangible tension.

On a low sad wall, not far from our compound, a big-headed agama lizard, which just a few days previously had wooed and won the affections of a naïve female virgin with lies and false promises, was shunning the new bride's demands for love and sex. Far away in the market, where the odour of dirty sweat commingled with the amalgam of all the stenches from the one-thousand-and-one food items displayed openly in the blazing sun, houseflies, which normally outnumbered the sellers and buyers by five hundred to one, stayed away in fear of their lives.

I sat in a sofa in our lounge, trying to appear calm. My wife sauntered in, distressed but doing her utmost to hide her discomfort. She slumped beside me. I was tempted to make a few comments but decided against it. I noticed that her palms were sweating and that she was shaking slightly as she began to speak.

"What have you decided? I think we have to make a decision pretty fast. The situation is getting quite precarious". She had been waiting anxiously for two months for me to make a decision. Now the tension seemed to have reached its climax.

"Do you really mean we shall leave all this behind? And how are we going to survive if we get back to the east? . I never learnt to farm, you know".

"I think we have to think of our safety first". There was no suggestion that she doubted my ability to make a rational decision in a crisis. She continued: "If you listen to the radio, you can understand that the situation is getting worse. Many people have fled. Even Ogbo left this morning". I quickly made a point of correction: Ogbo, a very close friend of our family, only sent his family down to the east, and had since returned to the city.

She remained undaunted. "Perhaps it will be a wise thing to do like Ogbo and send down the kids to their grand parents in the east. Then you and I can decide if we want to continue taking the risk of being here".

I had a ready answer for this, but as I moved to verbalise the reply, some loud and impatient knocks were heard on our main gate. My open mouth remained open. My wife stiffened in decided anxiety. A chunk of cobweb fell from the ceiling with an ear-shattering bang. Certain ghostly footfalls became deafening in their staccato. I was submitting to my fear of tragedy. Then I recovered myself. I remembered where I was. I remembered the situation in the country. I remembered the knocks on the gate.

My immediate reaction was to think whether I

remembered to lock the gate. I was certain, or almost certain, that I did. The gate through the gigantic walls of our elegant duplex structure was always locked - especially after the past couple of months. I began to sweat. My mouth opened again. As the MAN of the house, I stood up, as was expected, to confront the threat to the household. My legs felt wobbly and tired, telling me they were too exhausted to carry my body. The knocks continued with an indifferent and indecent fury.

Quickly, I ran upstairs and changed my pyjamas. I put on a pair of shorts and looked at my watch: twenty past two. I threw up the mattress on my bed, searching for the penknife that I had hidden underneath it for self-protection since the crisis began in early January 1966. Relieved that it was still where I had hidden it, I stuffed it into the pocket of my shorts and, the whole process having taken less than twenty seconds, re-emerged in the living room. My wife was still over-whelmed by fear. She was pacing up and down in transparent panic.

Without saying a word, I headed straight to our main gate. My wife trudged nervously behind. At the main entrance gate to the twenty-metre high wall that barri-caded our compound, I stopped and shouted, with an inflated fury and confidence: "Who is that?" Warm water trickled from my palms. An electric chill circulat-ed maliciously through my nervous system. Then a bel-lowing voice, familiar and non-aggressive replied: "It is I, Lieutenant Udo. It is very urgent".

I was visibly relieved, as was my wife. Lieutenant Udo was from the same Ibo ethnic group as we were, and a good friend of the family.

I told him to come in, and unlocked the gate. He was wearing civilian attire, an indication that he was visiting under some form of anonymity. The worried looks on his oval face portended danger.

"Chief, you must leave for the east immediately. It is no longer safe for us. Myself, I am leaving immediately. No Ibo is safe here".

"But..."

"Sir, you must leave immediately. With your family. No Ibo is safe here".

"But the Yorubas have nothing against us. This is between us and...".

"Order from the Federal Government. They say it is between the rest of the country and us. Can't you see? They arrested and detained all the Ibo students at the University of Ibadan last night. The other students are protesting at the army barracks. My suggestion is to seize the moment now and disappear. Don't waste a second. The next hour may be too late, sir".

Then he about-turned, soldierly, and hurried back to his home.

2

After he had gone, we began to panic. Self-preservation is truly the strongest human instinct. There was little thought about what we had, or what we would leave behind. We could perceive death outside our house, and were silently resolved to leave before he found the entrance.

For three or four minutes my wife gathered some of her most treasured personal effects, mainly clothes. She then ran to the room where I was silently and sadly doing my own packing. I was organising my financial affairs; cash, bank accounts, details of those who owed me, and other items with potential monetary value. My wife was crying.

"What is wrong? We are already packing and we will leave in the next ten minutes. Why these tears now?".

"I wonder where Lucy has gone with Obi. I warned her not to be far away from the house. We cannot leave without Obi. No, we cannot". She spoke each sentence between fresh outbursts of sobs.

"No, we can't", I concurred. After a while, I added: "I'm sure they will soon be back. Before we finish, they will be back. So don't worry".

My attempts at the role of a confidence builder evidently didn't work. She looked at me as if I were the most uncaring man in the world, and without speaking dashed out of the building in search of Lucy, the house-help, and our ten-month old son Obi. Minutes after she had gone I could still hear her sobs.

She came back about ten minutes later, alone. She suddenly looked haggard and unkempt. It was as if she had aged 15 years in as many minutes.

She was still crying, tears streaming down her cheeks: "My Obi, My Obi".

"Did you look in Barrister Ogene's home? In Nze's home? In Echo's home? They must be in one of these places". We lived in Bodija, an affluent area beyond the suburbs of Ibadan. Being a former-senior-civil-servant-turned-prosperous-businessman, our two children (Obi and his elder brother, Agada) interacted mostly with the children of the well-heeled in city.

"I have looked everywhere..." she started, but broke into a deep-throated cry. I placed my right hand on her head. For a long minute, I said nothing, just letting her know that I was there for her. Her head was bowed, and was leaning against my shoulders. I tried to smooth the tidal rise and fall of her back as she sobbed. I knew she needed to know that I cared. With the back of my hand, I began to wipe away her tears. After a while, I said to her, "I have finished packing. I mean what I consider the most important things. I have put all of them in the car. Get into the car and we will try to look for Obi. And Lucy. I am sure they are in the vicinity. I am sure of that. We will pick them up and then drive straight home... south of the Niger from where we came".

She didn't protest, and she didn't try to go and change her clothes. The Peugeot 403 saloon had already been brought out of the garage. Its fuel tank was, as always, full to the brim. She hopped onto the front seat and made Agada sit on her lap.

We drove round the city of Ibadan for nearly an hour looking for Obi and Lucy. We looked in all the likely places without success. The air was thick with tension, which was growing thicker by the minute. Students of the University of Ibadan were driving round the city with a loud speaker, threatening mayhem and bloodshed if their arrested colleagues were not released within twenty-four hours. More soldiers than usual were on the streets, their rifles cocked, and wearing menacing looks. Many armoured tanks were rolled out around the army barracks. Most of the cars and lorries were carrying Ibos, the faces of whom betrayed their eagerness to escape from the threatening cascade that they could all smell and touch. Many of them recognised us as we drove around in search of my son and househelp. Some of them wondered loudly why we had not yet left the city. After all, we had our own car! The expressions on the faces of these fleeing Ibos added another dimension to the deadly stench that hung menacingly in the October clouds of Ibadan. But we did not give up.

We continued our search, driving around in the town, and ending up at our Bodija home at least ten times - just in case they came back behind our backs. Suddenly we began hearing shots. We did not know exactly what those shootings were for. But that was it. With my wife and child we prayed for God to protect our Obi, and our house-help, wherever they might be. We cried aloud as we prayed inside the car, demanding to know from God why He was allowing this to happen to us. Finally, we resigned our fates and those of Obi and Lucy to His hands, and started the car again.

Unconsciously I looked at my watch. It was two minutes past four. I engaged the gear and headed east. So began the 400-kilometre journey to Ezinma, east of the river Niger.

3

It was probably destiny. How else could this be explained? Why should Lucy choose to vamoose with Obi at that critical time? Hadn't she heard us complaining of the situation in the country? Didn't she know that as an Ibo, she had to be extra careful? What was she really up to?

The whole tragedy unfolded this way: Obi had been crying uncontrollably. Lucy, the house-help, immediately appeared from the boys' quarter, where she was instructed to be at all times, unless needed by my wife or myself. From experience, she knew that when Obi was in one of his moods, strapping him on her tiny back and taking a long walk always helped. Therefore, standing before my wife, she didn't wait to be told to offer her back.

The morning air welcomed them reluctantly as they left the compound. The wind, without any warning, suddenly became rude, and tried unsuccessfully to raise Lucy's torn skirt past her lap. In the big mango tree nearby, some birds began giggling at the wind's erotic interest in a twelve year-old house girl.

Outside the view of everyone, Lucy lowered Obi from her back. He cried in protest. She looked from left to right and, seeing no one, began: "Shut up!". It was an order, barked with all the bottled anger that was buried in the recesses of her soul. But Obi was too young to understand and protested vehemently by crying louder. Again she quickly looked around before continuing: "You want my back, eh? How much food did your mother give me this morning to make this back strong enough for you?"

Obi's cry became even louder.

"Come on, shut up your dirty mouth!" she commanded, pulling him by the left ear, and giving him two knocks on the head at the same time. Just then she sighted some people coming from her left. Quickly, she offered her back to him and began another lullaby, shuffling her soot-black legs rhythmically as she sang.

As Obi fell asleep on her back, Lucy began to think fast. She had heard her madam many times in the past few days soliloquise about the need to get out of the city. She had also noticed her master becoming more and more withdrawn as he sought solace in the unthreatening company of his silent thoughts. She knew it had much to do with what my wife and I always referred to as the `situation', and that sooner or later we would have to return` to our ethnic homeland in the east. Of course, she didn't expect us to give her any notice and decided therefore to move fast before it became too late for her. The idea of losing all her three years' savings sent shudders to her spines.

She began to trot. On the road junction, she looked from left to right, and not seeing any face she could recognise, she took the path to the right. She knew he would be home. He had himself told her that he was ill with malaria. She figured he would be recuperating. She also calculated that his master would be in their workshop at the Dugbe market, and that his master's wife would also be in the market where she sold dry fish. She felt that this was her best chance of getting her money back - before it became too late.

She began to walk faster. After about twenty minutes,

she came to a narrow path separating the Bodija area from the poor Gbeti quarters. She paused to look around, and then broke into a run towards Gbeti. Obi bobbed up and down but, after snorting out a long whine, somehow went back to sleep again.

She was right in her calculation. The mud-walled compound seemed deserted. She entered the premises like a ghost, knowing where her Sunday would be. The small hut, annexed to the main building, was a round, decrepit structure which seemed happy to be hiding behind the main house. She tapped gently on the narrow door.

A young man's voice, sleepy and sickly, answered: "Yes Sir". Lucy pushed the door back and entered.

Sunday exclaimed: "ha!" and joyfully sprang up from the narrow, wooden bed, which contained only a mat.

" Take out the child from your back and put him on the bed ", Sunday said, offering his help.

"No. I won't stay long. I won't stay long". Her protestations were very vehement.

"Is anything wrong?" His eyes immediately focused on her stomach. In his eyes, it seemed to have become a little larger. Silently, he began to panic.

"I think we may be leaving back for the east anytime from now", she said slowly, interrupting his train of thought.

He heaved a sigh of relief.

"Why?" he inquired after a while, in honest curiosity. He was Yoruba, and therefore couldn't quite understand.

"I don't know. Of course, it may have something to do with the present situation".

"Too bad. Is there really any cause for...I mean are the Ibos in danger here? I don't think...." He was per-

14

haps thinking of himself, of losing his *sugar girl*, but Lucy's voice interrupted: "I have come to collect that thing, since I do not know when we will be leaving. It may be today. It may be tomorrow. I don't know".

Sunday was surprised. He opened his mouth and scratched his head. With a measured calmness, he sat down on the bed, and said slowly, "It Isn't possible now. You know I don't keep it here. I told you it's my maternal uncle who keeps it. We need to give him some notice before we can take it".

The thirty Nigerian pounds she had given him to keep for her was an accumulation of the cents and pennies she had saved by pinching from the money she was given to buy some food condiment or other. She had also opened her madam's purse on a number of occasions but always had the good judgement to take only as little as would not be noticed.

Initially, this little fortune was kept in a hole in her room - at a spot constantly covered by her mat. Within a couple of months, the fortune had grown too much for its hiding hole, which made her constantly nervous whenever someone entered her room. So when she began her secret affair with the twenty-four-year-old-Sunday, she decided to utilise him as her banker.

"You have to find a way of getting it from him. Can't you go to his shed in the market?" she asked, after thinking it over for some seconds.

"You do know that I am ill? What if my master sees me?"

"So you want me to leave for the east without the money? Is that the way you love a woman? Since you started doing it with me, I have never asked you for money. And now you can't even give me back what is mine". Tears were clouding her eyes. Sunday got up from the bed and went closer to where she was standing and tried to show some affection by using the back palm of his left hand to clean off the gathering tears. She pushed away his hand. He stood still and thought for two seconds.

"OK, I will go", he finally announced.

She said nothing.

He tried to caress her cheeks. This time she didn't resist. The hovering hand finally rested on her putative breasts.

"No", she said, and pushed away his hand.

"Why not? You also refused the last time".

"I don't want to.... I don't feel like".

"Why?". There was a suppressed anger in his voice.

After a while, he said sarcastically, "OK, I also don't feel like running to Dugbe market when I am ill".

Tears immediately began streaming down her cheeks. Sunday sat on the bed, sulking.

"Maybe next time. There won't be time for it now. I have been away for too long. Maybe they are already wondering where I have gone to". He said nothing. There was silence, except for the noisy pounding of Lucy's heartbeat and Obi's deep snoring. "Can't you understand that I have been gone for too long? Maybe they are already looking for me. Think of the time it will take us.... Think also of the time it will take you to get to Dugbe market".

"It won't take that long. As soon as we finish, I will run off to get the money while you go home. When I get it, I will bring it to...."

"No, I don't want you to do that", she interrupted.

"I don't mean bringing it inside your home. I will dig a hole behind the mango tree, hide it there, and cover the hole with grasses. Then at your convenience, you will go and pick it up".

Sunday remained insistent on his demand, and on

his conditionality. After a while she realised that *doing it* was perhaps the only way of getting the money. The choice was therefore pretty simple: do it or forgo your little fortune. The choice for her was crystal clear.

It was during the act that Sunday heard the jingles of his master's bicycle bell. He quickly jumped up and hitched up his pants. He knew that the only way of preventing his master from coming to his room was to get to the main house and present himself. That might mean acting as if his illness had gone, which would be cheery news for his master. Sunday knew he might be asked to get to the shop immediately. He thought about this for a while, and quickly resolved that it was a much better option than the discovery of his *sugar girl*.

"Stay here and don't come out until he is gone. I am sure he won't stay long. Don't allow that child to wake up and cry". Sunday's order was made in a hushed tone as he dashed out to welcome his master.

The master stayed long. Sunday told him that he felt a little better, which he was glad to hear. As he tidied up the lounge, his master who was reclining on one of the two armchairs there fell asleep shortly afterwards.

He knew his master was not a deep sleeper.

Lucy was by this time sobbing and cursing herself for making the visit at all. Sunday, meanwhile, was sweating profusely, wondering why his master had chosen to stay so long on this particular day.

4

They were not liberated until five o'clock. As she ran home, she had a feeling of great foreboding: lorries bundled people and belongings like packs of sardines, and she felt that those passing to and fro looked at her with suspicion. People were leaning out of their windows with expressions of sadness. What the hell was happening? Even the clouds above her seemed many shades darker than usual, an ominous colour that signalled more than imminent rain, rather a sign of Mother Nature's clear displeasure at the actions of man. Lucy also noted that the songs from the birds were closer to laments, warped with sorrow.

She was absorbed in a combined feeling of foreboding and fantasy that completely overwhelmed her. In her separate world, she kept thinking of a credible lie to explain her long absence from home:

While she was outside the compound singing a lullaby to Obi, an army vehicle had pulled up beside them. Before she knew it, she and Obi were pushed into the vehicle, driven to an unknown place by the two non-Ibo soldiers in the jeep, and released only when an Ibo soldier intervened.

Yes, that would fit the general frame of the "situation", she thought. She was just beginning to feel a little calmer when she heard a voice:

"Stop!" The no-nonsense tone of the voice brought her back to the real world. She was by now only about three meters away from their compound.

Lucy couldn't figure out which of the four-armed soldiers standing in front of her had given the command. Then again, she was simply too frightened to care.

"Who are you?" It was the tallest of the four soldiers who asked this. His accent was unmistakably Yoruba. Lucy stood frozen, with Obi still firmly strapped on her back. The soldier who asked the question began to advance towards her while the other three followed him behind, their rifles cocked. "I say who are you?"

"My name is Lucy. I live here".

"You live here?"

"Yessir".

"Where is your *oga*?"

"I don't know".

"And where have you been?" the shortest of the four men asked.

Silence.

The four soldiers exchanged glances, and as if by some silent transmission of shared feelings, the lines on their foreheads began to disappear, giving their faces a friendlier ambience. One of the soldiers began to explain: "Some soldiers have been posted to protect prominent Ibo citizens in the town. He and his colleagues are asked to come and protect the owner of this compound. They understand he is called chief Ogwu. They have managed to gain entrance to the compound, but from the look of things, it seems that chief Ogwu and his family have vamoosed. But they choose, all the same, to guard the house against possible vandalism by fanatics. "

"No, they haven't left. They won't leave without us". Tears were freely flowing down her cheeks. Obi, though too young, appeared to understand everything and in no time burst into an uncontrollable cry. The soldiers began to console the two in turn.

"I suspect they got dead-scared and therefore went into hiding. I am sure they will come out soon to look for you. They can't possibly leave the town without their son and you. So relax. Everything will be alright soon". She cast a quick glance at the tallest of the soldiers as he said these reassuring words. She did not want to spoil the soothing effects of those words by remembering that just two minutes before this officer had talked to her in a most menacing manner.

She sat down as she was instructed to do, on a bench beside the gate to the compound, and began the long wait. Meanwhile, in God's own sky, darkness continued its gradual but inexorable spread over the fast fading sunlight. In the distance, the dusk was being enveloped by a mystical quality, as insects chirruped busily.

At around nine o'clock that evening, a heavy motorcycle pulled up in front of the compound. The four soldiers, as if suddenly pricked by a charged electronic device, sprang up and stiffened to attention. Almost simultaneously they offered a salute.

The four soldiers relaxed their stiffened bodies as the man saluted back and began to advance towards them. They spent about two or three minutes talking in whispers. Then the man returned to his motorbike.

From where she was sitting in the darkness, Lucy observed the military etiquette with indifference. She was carrying the sleeping Obi on her lap, and was too exhausted to follow any line of thought. The tallest of the four soldiers, who was perhaps also the highest ranking, approached her.

"It doesn't seem that they are going to come out of hiding tonight". Sobs and more sobs. Obi stirred from his sleep, gave two mouthfuls of cries, and quickly went back to sleep. "We just received instructions to go home".

The man placed his big hand on her narrow shoulders, and began to console her.

"You understand the current situation in the country now," he began, speaking in the same pidgin English that they had been using to communicate all along.

"You know that General Aguiyi Ironsi, the Ibo-born head of state, was murdered in this very town. You know that there is a lot of tension in this country now. The Ibos are talking of seceding from the Federation. The Northerners want to fight against this. The position of the Yorubas on this is not yet very clear. That is why the Ibos here are afraid. Many of them have fled back to the east while some have gone into hiding. I think that your master is one of those who went into hiding".

An owl began hooting in the distance. Obi jerked, opened his eyes for two brief seconds, farted, and went back to sleep. The man continued.

"I think what is happening now is a shame to the whole country and to all of us. But I am supremely confident that the situation is under control".

Lucy said nothing.

"I don't think it is safe to allow you to spend the night here. Do you know any family you can spend the night with?" Lucy shook her head. The man closed his eyes, placed his right hand over his face, and thought quickly for about thirty seconds. "You can come and spend the night in my home. Tomorrow, we will try to find out where they are hiding". His three colleagues nodded their approval to the gesture. Lucy stood up lazily, her legs seemingly too weak to carry her frame. She shoved Obi to her back, and strapped her firmly there, with a piece of cloth. The man led the way, chatting with his colleagues in a voice only slightly above a whisper as they walked. Lucy trudged behind.

---

1. pidgin name for a master.

5

Leaving Ibadan without my son was a huge blow. It was even more agonising for my wife, Teresa, who cried for hours and refused to be consoled.

Lucy's parents visited to offer their commiserations. They cried, although it was difficult to make out if their crying and wailing were for their daughter they lost, or as apologies to us.

I suppose the latter was the case, especially after the way Teresa told the story in the village. The blame was mounted squarely at the feet of Lucy, with "housemaids of nowadays" and a shake of the head the standard responses. And they were many listeners, for Teresa told the story over and over again to any one willing to listen.

The civil war between the east and the rest of the country broke out a couple of months after we arrived in our village. With this, the agonising about Obi receded, in time, to the background. Instead, we became pre-occupied with survival.

The new Republic of Biafra offered me a job as a relief officer for my village. The post made me in charge of all the food relief for the village. My wife called that a God-sent job, and a local diviner in the village said that Obi was the price I would pay to survive the war. Obi was dead. She was very emphatic about that.

The visit to the soothsayer about Obi's fate wasn't my first time of consulting those who claimed to know what destiny had in store for everyone. As a young bare-feet lad with frequent sores at the corners of my mouth, such visits to diviners were quite common. There were always things very puzzling to my mother, who, like most other people in the village, admitted to not being able to see beyond the ordinary and the human. Such puzzles always centred on questions like: Is this child going to survive? Is he/she an ogbanje[1]? Are there people in the village who will rather see the child dead? Was anyone responsible for his/her illness? Why are they having poor harvests? Who will their daughter/son marry? A reptile entered their compound in a funny way, and at an odd hour, what does that mean? One of their cocks crows constantly at mid-day or mid-night, what are the gods trying to say?

In my village in those days, the soothsayers (or *medicine men* as some called them) always had the answer. And there were always some sacrifices involved, which often made me suspicious, though I never mustered enough courage to speak of my doubts. By the time I qualified as a primary school teacher in the late fifties, I had totally stopped all those nocturnal visits to them. I actually began to loathe them. I had become a Christian, you know, and had, at one point, actually toyed with the idea of becoming a Catholic priest.

As a teacher, I still kept close to Catholic religious practices, which was not always easy, especially when many of the nationalists agitating for independence kept telling us that Christian religion was a form of cultural imperialism. Those of us practising it at that time therefore often felt like sell-outs. But nevertheless, we held onto the belief and cherished the status that in many ways came with it.

***

Independence offered many possibilities for people with some education like myself. With the departure of the colonisers, a lot of positions suddenly became vacant in the civil service. The nationalists were all eager to Nigerianise every aspect of civil and political life. I quickly got a position in the Western Region's civil service at Ibadan as a senior administrative officer and this opened my eyes to new realities. As a teacher, we believed that our reward would be in heaven. In the civil service, the belief was that people's reward was (and ought to be) right here on earth. So many of us admittedly did quite a number of funny things just to get this immediate reward.

A few years after independence, I was sent on a one-year diploma course in public administration at a polytechnic in East London. On returning to the civil service, I was promoted to a post where the ultimate responsibility for awarding most of the contracts in my division lay with me. Believe me, this was a much-envied job. It was widely believed that any one occupying that position had to fortify himself with strong *juju* because of the fierce jealousy and envy which it generated. I only relied on prayers.

Many people (friends and admirers, I believe) who felt that I was not properly *fortified* quickly began advising me to quit the job in my own interest. I had been in this job for less than two years and I really liked it. It was such a lucrative position that I loathed any idea of quitting. However, though I was a Christian, I never pretended not to fear the malevolence of certain mystical forces. I also did not doubt that my colleagues were capable of mobilising such forces against me. Already, they were openly flaunting ethnic sentiments against me.

One Tuesday morning, I walked into my office. My mind was on something else. I couldn't remember exactly in which dream world I found myself, or what my status was in that world. Suddenly my eyes caught something very terrifying - a giant lizard sitting comfortably and leisurely on my chair. I was dead-scared.

The same day I decided to look for a reputed *jujuman* in the village for his advice. This was actually the first time I was doing such a thing since I converted to Christianity. His advice to me was straightforward: people were after my life so I should quit my job immediately.

I did so the following day and immediately turned my energies to business. I went into contracts and transport businesses and became very successful. I also kept contacts with the *babalawo*[2] who advised me to quit my civil service job.

Not long afterwards, I began to prefix *chief* to my name. I was now formally addressed as *chief Pete Gutter Ogwu*. My friends and admirers affectionately called me *chief P.G.O.*

Sometime in May 1966, one of the guys who worked under me when I was in the civil service ran to my home. Rashid was so much in a hurry to relay the message to me that he almost forgot to bow properly to me in the Yoruba fashion of showing respect to one's elders. I immediately knew that something either too pleasant or too unpleasant was in the offing.

"What is wrong, Rashid?" I asked, taking him by the hand, and leading him into my house.

"Sir, I think they want to probe you, sir".

"Probe me?" I asked in wonderment.

"Yessir. I think it may be jealousy. You know every one knows that you have become even more successful since you resigned".

I said nothing to that comment. I tried to appear very calm. I knew that when I was in the civil service...well, I did receive a number of *gifts* after awarding some contracts. But then I also knew that almost every one else in the service also received one form of "gift" or the other for services or help rendered to others. I did not want to pretend that if I was probed, I would be found innocent.

***

He welcomed me to his little thatch hut that night and listened without interruption as I narrated the story. I told him that what I wanted was not to be found innocent when probed but not to be probed at all, full stop. When I finished, he closed his eyes for three long minutes, and in his lotus position, looked every inch a Tibetan Buddhist in transcendental meditation. When he finally opened his eyes, the only words he muttered to me were, "see you tomorrow evening." That was a dismissal, but I could read from his facial countenance that he took the matter very serious.

The following evening he gave me some concoctions. He asked me to drink one glass of it everyday - for thirty days. I can still remember the stinky smell of that concoction. He also gave me a string. I was to wear it around my waist and make love to any mad woman whose madness had reached the stage where she walked the streets naked. The thought of this nearly drove me to tears. I began pleading that this be substituted with something more decent. He answered that it wasn't within his powers to do so, and that if I really wouldn't like to be probed, then I would simply have to do it - and fast.

***

Not too far from the area of Ibadan where we lived, on the road that led to Ojor, I used to see a mad woman.

Every one called her Tokunbo. She always went about stark naked with flies often hovering around her buttocks. The thought of doing such a thing with her sent shudders to my veins. But then, did I really have any choice?

That same afternoon I drove past the area. I saw Tokunbo sleeping under the shed, with flies as usual hovering around her. There was a bicycle repair shed about fifty metres away from where she was sleeping. I took note of this as I sped past in my car.

I returned to the spot about eight o'clock that evening. Tokunbo was gone. The bicycle shop was also empty and there were only a few passers-by. I parked my car and began walking to-and-fro, hoping that she would appear miraculously. She didn't. I was about to give up hope when suddenly I saw a tall figure swaggering towards me. I stopped and moved to the edge of the road and pretended that I was urinating. Soon the figure came close enough. It was Tokunbo. But Satans! There were about two other figures approaching from the same direction as she!

I said "hi" to her but she ignored me and kept walking. After sauntering for about twenty metres, she stopped, and went and lay in the bicycle shed.

As soon as the road was clear of thoroughfare, I went to her and flashed out a pound note. I showed her this under my torchlight, and her face beamed with smiles. She stood up to take the money from me but I dragged her to the bush. Within five minutes, it was all over.

About three months later rumour began circulating that Tokunbo, the mad woman, had become pregnant. Every decent person, including my humble self, angrily condemned the heartless and shameless man who did such an awful thing to her.

My greatest fear after this was that Tokunbo might

recognise me or that my *babalawo* friend would let it out that I was the likely culprit. I was still worried about how to handle Tokunbo and the *babalawo* when we fled Ibadan. So in that sense, our flight from Ibadan was a relief for me from all those trouble.

---

1. children who are believed to be members of a supernatural cult. According to the belief,such kids deliberately cause their parents sorrows by dying at a pre-determined age only to be born to die again. According to the belief, such a cyle of birth and premature death can be stopped only through the intervention of appropriate village priests who could cut off their links with their cult.
2. Yoruba word for a ju-juman.

6

Though Tokunbo's pregnancy attracted quite a lot of compassion and outrage, it also drew a similar dosage of ridicule. The youngsters especially loved to tease her whenever no adult was around. They would ask her how she felt when the man was doing it, whether she enjoyed it, and who the man really was. Tokunbo usually fought back - verbally. Sometimes she damned them by placing her hands on either side of her dirty buttocks, and exposing her arsehole to her teasers. The naughty youngsters especially loved this, and did all they could, whenever they could, to provoke her into this inverted pornography. Finally, she could no longer stand the torment and moved to Bere, a ghetto quarter of the city, which was quite some distance from Bodija.

In mid-May 1967, Tokunbo gave birth to a bouncing baby girl. On the night of the birth, it rained heavier than it had done in living memory.

It has remained a mystery to this day how Tokunbo delivered her child. The morning after the terrifying downpour, the inhabitants of Bere woke up to see Tokunbo carrying a baby smeared in blood. No one had any idea if she managed it all on her own or not. However, the dry blood on her legs and hands and on the baby, made many believe that it most probably had been a solo effort. A good-natured old woman who sold bean balls, and on whose stall the delivery had taken place, eventually forced her to wash herself and the baby. But Tokunbo would hear none of her offer to adopt the child. Very afraid that the child would be forcibly taken away from her, she withdrew from Bere, and moved into Dugbe market - some distance away. There, in the middle of the market, under the shade of the big mango tree, she made her home. Her calculation was simple: being in the middle of the market would deter any one from stealing her child from her. Who said that mad people are not rational?

Despite her precaution, what she feared most happened anyway. This was less than two weeks after she moved to live in the market. It happened this way: it was late in the evening and almost everyone had left the market for their homes except the loafers and one or two others of Tokunbo's kind. A Peugeot 404 saloon car with a bold Red Cross insignia pulled up beside her. The child, very emaciated and obviously sick, was on her lap, gasping for air. She clutched more tightly to the child as the car pulled up beside her. She was sensing danger. A plump, middle-aged woman came out of the car and walked to Tokunbo.

"Your child is sick. We have to take her from you. We will bring her back as soon she has become well". She said this in a gentle and friendly voice, but Tokunbo reacted angrily, cursing and threatening. She tried to bite the lady's outstretched hand. The woman tried to explain, but Tokunbo was in no mood to listen. She was determined not to allow this to happen. She had allowed other people to be as they please- why won't others do the same to her? Suddenly an idea dropped into her mind. She would run away. She would run into the forest where she would be free from people who laughed or sympathised with her.

She quickly sprang up. Before she could make a

move, the Red Cross lady grabbed the baby. She tried to fight back but the lady pushed her back, and quickly got into the car with the child. She closed the door with a bang, and Tokunbo chased it as it sped away. She cursed and cried as she ran after the white car until it disappeared over the hill. Finally, she slumped, exhausted and overwhelmed. The following day, she was found dead.

The baby was taken to the St. Anthony's hospital, about one and half kilometres away from the spot where she was taken away from her mother. She was hospitalised for one week. On discharge, she was taken to the orphanage near the University of Ibadan.

She was there for ten days before she was adopted.

7

One of the urgent problems when I moved to Lagos with my family was how to earn the daily bread necessary to maintain my family. Before long, I got a teaching job in one of the local secondary schools.

I taught African history to class four and five students. The salary wasn't fantastic, but it was good enough relative to the prevailing standard in the country at that time. I could reasonably support my family, and even amassed some savings. Soon, I had saved enough money to repair my Peugeot 404 saloon car, which had broken down during the war but was never repaired due to lack of spare parts.

Shortly after putting the vehicle back on the road, I got involved in a serious motor accident. It had happened this way: I was on my way one early morning to the secondary school where I taught. I had been on the job for about six months, with my initial enthusiasm and gratitude for the job on the wane. In place of the initial gratitude for having a job and the means of supporting my family, I had begun to long for my pre-war economic well-being, social standing and respect. My teaching job was clearly incapable of offering me any of these.

I was absent-minded as I drove, with my thoughts jostling between a deep-seated bitterness and a desire to think creatively in order to get out of this morass. I was little more than a physical body behind the steering wheel, my mind and soul being kilometres away.

Suddenly, there was a very noisy, crashing sound behind and in front of me. Swearing and cursing was followed by silence. Black silence. I regained consciousness the following evening and found myself in a sparkling white hospital bed. There were bandages on my head, left hand, and both legs. My wife and children were there when I opened my eyes. They were the ones who explained it all to me: I had been involved in a ghastly car accident.

I was hospitalised for five weeks. My car - or what was left of it- had been towed to my home. My God! How could anyone have survived from such a wreck? It appeared that someone had hit me from behind and I had hit someone in front of me. The car really looked squeezed. My wife said that both the guy who had hit me, and the woman whom I hit, had died in the accident.

I was very depressed for many months afterwards. My teaching job suddenly no longer seemed a disgrace. Rather, I became more and more grateful to God that I survived the accident. I was also deeply thankful that my family and I survived the war, that we were able to leave Ibadan safely before the war broke out, and that no member of my nuclear or extended family was affected by the *kwashiokor* epidemic during the war. Suddenly the accident made me begin to think of worldly cravings as mere vanity. Not that I had not thought about this before. Of course I had. There has always been, inside my soul, a poor, deeply religious thing struggling to rise above the overpowering pull of the earthly and the material.

I quickly concluded that the car accident was a sign and a warning from God to me. Did I not promise before I left my village for Lagos that I was going to get closer to Him? After seven months in Lagos, did I ever make any effort to fulfil my promise to Him? No. Rather, all those unworldly thoughts with which I had left my village for Lagos had disappeared with the first whiff of success.

As I sat reflecting over my life, and feeling religious, the melody of a very apt song slipped into my soul.

God moves in a mysterious way,
His wonders to perform....

I was humming this song, happy with myself, and not caring a hoot about the world, when my wife and children entered my bedroom. My happiness infected every one in the room.

Three weeks later, the Back-to-God church was born in our two-bedroom flat in Surulere, Lagos.

8

Lucy and the army officer arrived safely at the narrow, one-room apartment in the army barracks. It took them about thirty minutes of walking to get there. She had, on the way, learnt that the man's name was Ade, that he was a sergeant in the infantry division of the Nigerian army, and that he was a bachelor.

"Make yourself comfortable". The sergeant didn't look especially proud of his flat. Lucy took in everything in the apartment with a single glance.

The floor was bare and dirty. There was, at the centre of the rectangular room, a low stool that badly needed cleaning. A tiny transistor radio on the small window in the room was the only modern gadget in the apartment.

She unfastened the sleeping Obi from her back. For a moment, she silently felt grateful to Sergeant Ade for providing them refuge. She was too exhausted from too much thinking, too much worrying, and too much crying. She was also understandably hungry.

Sergeant Ade was fast with making the food - jollof rice that was cooked without meat, and served in flat, not-so-clean plates. Though just a housemaid, living in the relative comfort of our home had exposed her to better standards.

They ate the food. Sergeant Ade did his best to reassure her that everything would be all right by the following day. Lucy didn't know if he was lying or not. Somehow, she didn't care. All she needed at that time was a strong dose of assurance, and Sergeant Ade, it had to be said, was doing a good job of it.

The sergeant didn't feel bad that she was falling asleep while he was still talking to her. If he did, it didn't show on him. As soon as he noticed that he was talking to himself - and perhaps also to Obi who opened his sleepy eyes now and again only to quickly close them again, he went and prepared the six-spring bed in the room. He took Obi from her, and motioned her to the bed. Too exhausted and too sleepy, she obeyed the instruction like one under hypnosis.

She must have slept uncomfortably for close to two hours. Suddenly she had a feeling of big hands fumbling her thighs. She opened her eyes. Sergeant Ade was lying on the floor beside the bed. His right forefinger was placed across his tightly clenched lips. This was a sign that she must not scream or talk aloud.

"No", she muttered, clasping her thighs together.

"Don't talk. It is very late. The neighbours may hear you. You know the situation in the country now. If they discover that you are an Ibo, it may be dangerous for you", he whispered.

'No', she muttered again.

Obi reclined on the bed. The sergeant's facial expression became a little fiendish. Though she couldn't see his face in the darkness, she understood the full implications of his sudden ominous silence. She became stricken by fear and watched helplessly as he lifted Obi out of the bed, and onto the cushions on the floor. Quickly, he unbuttoned his trousers, took off his shirt, and asked her to create space for him in the bed. She obeyed, visibly frightened.

The following morning, Sergeant Ade, dressed in his starchy army uniforms and heavy black boots, left for work. He had promised that he was going to mobilise all the forces he could muster to smoke us out from wherever we might be hiding. He asked Lucy to remain indoors with Obi. The room must be very firmly locked, he instructed. The situation in the country was terrible. Therefore, no one - repeat no one- must know that she was staying in that apartment. When Sergeant Ade came back, he would knock on the door three times, and then call her by name. That would be the right-of-passage sign. It was, repeat, absolutely necessary for Lucy to observe it.

He returned in the evening with no cheering news. Her eyes were weary from too much worrying. She didn't know what to do but was too exhausted to give words to her sorrows. Obi was crying like hell. Lucy couldn't figure out why but felt it might have something to do with his missing us, his parents

Two more days passed without any news of us. The Sergeant felt concerned. He was worried about Lucy's deteriorating mood, and equally concerned about his job. What explanation should he give his superiors for keeping her and the child for so long in his home?

"Did you find out anything today?" she asked, while opening the door for him as he returned from work one day.

He didn't reply. He just slumped himself on the two-sitter couch with a noisy hiss of sorrow.

She repeated her question.

"Yes. But I am afraid it is not a good news".

Her face dropped in sadness. He was actually expecting a worse reaction. He paused and took a long, admiring glance at his heavy pair of boots. Then he started the phoney story:

"The Ogwus were driving recklessly as they fled the city. Honestly, they needn't have panicked. Unfortunately, they did. They collided with an oncoming lorry as they tried to overtake on a hill. May their soul rest in peace."

Tears began to stream freely down her cheeks. She didn't cry out loud. Just sobbing. The sergeant pretended to share her muffled sorrows. Obi looked curious.

The following evening, he returned from work with a huge, ebony black woman. She had the whitest set of teeth Lucy had ever seen in her life. Her broad smiles and cackling laughter reminded one of sunshine on a cloudless sky. She looked so happy with herself, and with the world. The woman stayed with them that evening for over two hours, chatting with the sergeant in their Yoruba language. Finally, she got ready to leave. The sergeant told Lucy that they would accompany the woman home that evening. Lucy didn't object.

In the woman's home, Sergeant Ade told Lucy that it would be best to leave Obi under the care of the woman "given the situation of Obi's parents". Also, "for her own security", Lucy must never tell any one about the arrangement. The woman would hide Obi, and take proper care of him, until they could figure out how to safely send them back to the east. Lucy would return home with him. She would henceforth claim to be married to him "for her own security". Lucy said nothing. The sergeant and the fat woman started making up a story for Lucy about how and when she got married to Ade. Obi farted. Outside, intermittent gunshots continued to disrupt the silence of the still, black night.

9

The Back-to-God Church wasn't really founded by the whole family. It was founded this way: It was about ten o'clock in the evening, sometime in late 1972. My wife and I were in our bedroom, praying. My youngest child Nkem, was deeply sleeping in the living room, occasionally smiling at God-knows-what. She often did this when she was sleeping. The first child, Agada was with us in the bedroom. We all closed our eyes as we prayed. Agada silently slipped out of the bedroom. We did not notice this. By the time we did, he was already conveniently asleep and was snoring deeply and noisily, cruising on the wings of the god of sleep.

My wife and I ignored this. We got lost in prayers. Suddenly we began feeling a certain chill. We interpreted this to be a sign of His presence in the room. We were shivering in religious ecstasy. The words of one of the prayers has remained indelible in my heart:

Oh, Lord, we your humble servants have gathered before you tonight. Lord, You have promised that when two or three are gathered together in Thine name, Thy will grant their requests. Fulfil now, Oh Lord, the desires and petitions of thy servants, which we are presenting before you.

Our most merciful Lord, we are deeply sorry for all our sins. We detest them above all things. We know that they deserve your dreadful punishment because they offend thy infinite goodness. We do not deserve to stand before your holy presence, being awash in sins....

We were interspersing our prayers with songs of praise. I loved those songs and we sang them with fervour. We were feeling very Godly, with our eyes closed. Our hands were spread out to the heavens. Our foreheads were creased - in wrinkles of concentration. Teresa, my wife, was initiating most of the songs.

The praying and singing finally ended. My wife and I sat down on the cabinet bed in the room. We began to review our performance.

"It was very nice. I really enjoyed it". It was very obvious the way she said it that she meant it.

"Me too. I really felt very godly."

"It is definitely the best prayers we have ever offered."

I agreed with her entirely.

"We should do it more often."

The idea had crossed my mind many times while we prayed. I simply answered: "Why not?"

The following night, we prayed and sang again, for close to three hours.

We were feeling nearly as good as we did the night before. Our souls were smeared with an eternal bliss, the kind of elation that comes only from unworldly preoccupations.

"What if we make this an evangelical movement?" Honestly, this question was asked in such a way that I was convinced that the Holy Spirit was asking it through me.

"How?"

"It doesn't have to be something big. Probably just you, me, and the children. Then occasionally we will invite some of our friends to pray with us".

There was silence. She looked clumsily at her fingers. Her head was bowed to the floor. She looked a little bit awkward and avoided an eye contact with me. A minute of silence passed. Finally, she answered: "it doesn't sound bad".

I felt relieved.

"What if we call this **BACK-TO-GOD CHURCH?**"

She said that the name sounded fine.

***

I woke up with a start less than two hours after we went to bed that night. My wife was sleeping gracefully beside me. The sound of her breathing was rhythmic and beautiful. For a while, I watched the gentle rise and fall of her chest as she slept. I shook her gently and kissed her on the mouth.

She opened her eyes. She was still visibly sleepy.

"Are you still sleeping?" I knew she was. I felt that it was the gentlest way of waking her up.

"You are not sleeping. Is anything wrong, chief?" Her voice sounded only half-asleep.

"Not especially. I only wanted to tell you something". The sound of my voice didn't suggest that the something I wanted to tell her was a bad one.

She sat up on the bed. She was now wide-awake and all ears. I stroked her gently on the face. Then I said: "I have just been thinking about this my title. I don't think I am still very excited about being exalted in this world. I mean I don't want to be called chief any more. Remember what the bible says: he that exults himself will be humbled, and he that humbles himself will be exalted. What will it profit me if I am called a chief in this world, and then have no place in heaven? I think the best exaltation is that which comes from God".

She didn't say anything. She placed her head on my hairy chest and held my right hand in warm affection. Sleepily, she muttered something about how much I

41

meant to her. Then she dosed off again.

***

The Back-to-God church quickly outgrew our bedroom. Our friends began coming every Sunday evening for bible study. We held this in our lounge. We had to respect the privacy of our bedroom, you know.

The arrangement was truly informal. I was especially careful not to present myself as the leader. Everyone present was always given a chance to lead the prayers and the hymn singing. Whenever we read and discussed the bible, each person's interpretation of the passage was always accepted as correct. If we did not feel that the explanation was correct, we never told the person so. We would rather say that the interpretation was "one way of looking at it".

Our friends obviously liked these bible studies and attended them regularly. Some started to come with their own friends, who in turn brought *their* own friends. Within six weeks, our lounge had become too small for our members. Soon, there was a consensus that we should meet more than once a week. Offertory also quickly became part of our meetings. Before we knew it, we had collected enough money to build a small church. It was a makeshift structure. Old planks and old corrugated sheets were used in place of blocks and cement. We were exceedingly proud of this structure.

10

Madam Cash lived well by local standards, and enjoyed the world of relative comfort in which she lived. The way she carried herself left no one in doubt about it.

Maria's father was a catechist, and was, in those days, considered very influential, for he was one of the few natives who enjoyed the company of the missionary white men.

Innocent Ajiboye's marriage to Maria was considered the most perfect marriage of the time, despite her being some eighteen years younger than him. Was she not the most educated girl in the village? Was she not the daughter of the catechist who interacted openly with the local white priest almost everyday? Was Innocent not the headmaster who, even visiting white men curtsied to? There was no perfection in life. Otherwise Innocent and Maria's marriage would have been that. Try as they might, they did not produce a child.

After many years of being the headmaster of a primary school, Innocent resigned his teaching job. He dabbled into politics and became filthy rich - almost overnight. He became more desperate to have kids, but Maria still had difficulties in conceiving. Cracks began to appear in the otherwise solid marriage. Rumours began flying around that he was making arrangements to re-marry.

Maria went about swearing to anyone who cared to listen that her husband would only re-marry over her dead body. One day Innocent Ajiboye died in his sleep. Many people in the village began suspecting foul play. They pointed accusing finger at Maria. But Maria, with the support of her ageing catechist father, fought back. She also won a protracted legal battle over the inheritance of her late husband's property.

She was soon conscious of being in a position of power and adopted a swaggering manner of walking to emphasise this knowledge. The nickname Madam Cash soon followed.

***

Madam Cash heard about sergeant Ade's story of an Ibo child and housemaid abandoned by fleeing Ibo parents. Her maternal instincts were aroused. She had never really considered adopting a child but the story deeply touched her. She suddenly began feeling that the child might be a gift from God.

Sergeant Ade, just like Maria, hailed from Ikire village. He was a scion of Innocent Ajiboye who helped him to get into the army. Ajiboye also influenced his posting to Ibadan because he wanted him to live close by. That was a way of letting Ade know he was monitoring his progress in the army. Sergeant Ade had remained ever grateful for this. He visited the Ajiboye family as often as two- three times a week. And whenever the Ajiboyes were on a trip where they felt the need for security or social splendour, sergeant Ade would gladly dress in his full military regalia and accompany them. He maintained his loyalty to the family even after Innocent had transited to the spirit world.

She agreed totally with him that it was improper to keep hiding the two Ibos in his apartment. They agreed that a better solution must be found and it didn't really take long before they decided that Madam Cash would take custody of Obi. The decision thrilled her.

Alone in her spacious living room, she began to sway herself in a joyous dance. Then abruptly she stopped dancing. A number of uncomfortable thoughts had dropped into her mind: what if the parents of the child later surface to demand their son back? What if they haven't actually fled the city? But supposing they have actually fled back to their Ibo homeland, won't they come back to look for their child as soon as the situation in the country becomes better? How long will it take the "current situation" in the country to return to normality?

An idea suddenly dropped into her mind in the midst of these labyrinths of thoughts: she would never let any one know how she got the baby. It would simply be a secret between her and sergeant Ade. She was absolutely convinced that sergeant Ade wouldn't talk about it to any one. Well, if he did, he certainly knew it wouldn't be in his own interest to do so. And if he didn't talk, and she kept quiet about it, how would the baby ever be taken away from her?

That afternoon, she called her housemaid and asked her to take a one-week leave. That wasn't the first time she had sent her on such an impromptu and compulsory leave. She often did that whenever she wanted to be with one of her teenage lovers.

She renamed the baby on the same day she acquired him. She gave him the Yoruba name of Femi, for no apparent reason. The story she spread was that she found the baby, stuffed in a carton, and abandoned at a corner of the road to Lagos. She was, she lied, driving to Lagos that fateful day, and was only a few kilometres into the journey when, suddenly, her instinct instructed her to pull over. She obeyed and, as she pulled off the road, the cry of a child was unmistakable.

Most of the people who heard this story bought it, or at least pretended to. Even her housemaid, on her return, appeared to believe it.

Madam Cash was quite happy with her new maternal role. Soon, she became convinced that nothing would ever take Femi away from her. Her only regret was that she allowed Lucy to come to her home with sergeant Ade. She feared that since Lucy was quite grown up, she might be able to trace her home as soon as the 'situation in the country' improved. Each time she thought of this, a pang of fear seized her.

She began to scheme for a way to make Lucy keep her mouth shut. Sergeant Ade was asked to put fear into her. She was told that the 'situation in the country' was so terrible for the Ibos that, if she told anyone the true story of how she came to live with sergeant Ade, there would be a likelihood of her being murdered by fanatics.

There was also the question of the two corporals who were there when sergeant Ade took Lucy and Obi home. After some brainstorming, they agreed on what sergeant Ade would tell them: he never really took them home that night. Actually, on their way, they ran into an Ibo man who was fleeing back to the east. The Ibo man knew chief Ogwu and offered to take them with him, which he willingly obliged.

Despite her precautions, the fear that Femi might be taken away from her occasionally haunted her. This fear got more nagging as she became more attached to the child.

It didn't take her very long to conceive a plan: Sergeant Ade and his wife, Lucy Ade, must be transferred to the Northern part of the country, where, the 'situation in the country' was even more terrible for the Ibos. Her calculation was that with their being very far away, the chance that Lucy would meet someone who knew chief Ogwu, and in whom she could confide in about the whereabouts of Obi, would be very small. In that way, she hoped to secure Femi for herself - as long as they both lived.

Sergeant Ade and Lucy were transferred to Kaduna and Madam Cash organised a send-off party for them. She cried during the party and told them how much she was going to miss them. She promised to do all in her power to bring them back to Ibadan as soon as possible.

Five days after they left Ibadan, Madam Cash received a telegram: Lucy and Sergeant Ade had been victims of a certain mob. They died.

On receiving the news, her first impulse was to celebrate. She was of course deeply sorry for the death of sergeant Ade and Lucy. But she somehow felt that their demise would put a permanent seal on her fear.

She was wrong for shortly afterwards, another fear began germinating in her mind. This was the fear that some of the soldiers at the Mokola military cantonment might start getting suspicious. Are they going to link her desire for Sergeant Ade to be transferred to the northern part of the country with his sudden death there? Exactly six months and three days after she took custody of Obi - and one month after the death of sergeant Ade and Lucy, Madam Cash could no longer live with the fear. She packed her bags and left for Lagos. Her rationale for the relocation was that Lagos had a better business future for her than Ibadan. Of course, she took Femi with her.

10

Tunde Johnson, Helle's husband, wanted children badly. He had already deferred to his wife's suggestion that they should wait a while and see what direction their relationship takes before having children. But for how long was he to wait?

Their first meeting was in the mid-1960s, in Copenhagen, Denmark. He had just completed his Master's degree in agricultural science from the University of London, and had stayed on for two weeks to enjoy the English capital's pubs and libraries. A chance meeting with a middle-ranking official in the Danish Foreign Ministry alerted him to the possibility of a research fellowship in Denmark. A subsequent application was successful. At the end of his fellowship, she decided to marry him and return with him to Nigeria-despite the vehement protestations of parents and friends.

Helle loved Nigeria deeply, the friendliness of its people and, she had to admit, also the admiring looks that came her way. In her country she was a nobody, a secretary in a small private company. In Nigeria, kids would run after her, calling her *oyibo*. Even the top layers of society were all too eager to be polite. She cherished this attention bestowed upon her by her skin pigmentation, though she pretended that she didn't.

By nature, Helle was quite compassionate. She often visited the sick and the downtrodden. One May afternoon in 1967, she came back from the secondary school where she taught biology. She was home earlier than usual, and experienced a sudden desire to visit an orphanage. She had never been to any orphanage in the country before; in fact she wasn't even aware that one existed within practical travelling distance. Her house-maid could not enlighten her, which served only to heighten her curiosity. It had now become a mission.

Such information was not hard to come by. They lived in the staff quarters of the University of Ibadan, and a short walk to the university's main gate was all it took to satisfy her curiosity. The tarred road that led to this gate was always busy with traffic, both the human and auto variety, and all she had to do was fall into step with someone and ask politely.

The first two people she asked had no idea but the third person, a well-dressed young student, was all too eager to impress. He knew everything about the two orphanages in the town, including when they were founded, and the approximate number of inmates in each. He even offered to take her to them but she politely declined.

She decided on the St. Ann's Motherless Babies Home. From the boy's description, it was farther away from the university than the St. Catherine's Motherless Babies Home. She did the twenty minutes walk without knowing or feeling it, being too absorbed about *the situation* in the country. She was so engrossed with her thoughts that she hardly noticed the many birds that seemed to be singing with increased verve that afternoon, as if they were trying to impress her.

She arrived at St. Ann's at the same time as a Peugeot saloon car bearing the insignia of the Red Cross. Instinctively, she felt that a new in-mate was being brought to the Home. She stood by the door of the Home and waited for the new arrival to disembark, ignoring the shouts of `oyibo!, oyibo* from the half-naked kids on the roadside.

Tokunbo's child emerged from the vehicle in the arms of a Red Cross official. Helle moved to them. The officials smiled and exchanged greetings with her. She asked how they came about the child, and when told, was greatly moved, with tears escaping uncontrollably from her eyes. The Red Cross officials allowed her to carry the child inside the Home.

On her way home, she thought a lot about the child. Although she always claimed she was not religious, and that she did not know whether she believed in God, she was often quick to admit that she believed in destiny. Or, as she always preferred to put it, in a supreme energy which pre-ordains and directs the affairs of all beings. Therefore, while walking home she could not help but wonder if fate had intervened. She thought very hard about it: why did she suddenly have the urge to visit an orphanage? Why did she choose to visit the St Ann's Home and not the St Catherine's Home, which was nearer to their residence? Why did they bring the baby to the Home just as she arrived there? What was the hidden message?

She returned to St Ann's three days later, still perplexed over the whole affair. She spent some forty minutes with the baby, and was none the wiser. The following week, she visited the Home four times and rapidly became attached to the baby. By the end of that week, her mind was made up.

Tunde's reaction stopped just short of hail, fire and brimstone. She didn't want a kid and yet she was prepared to adopt one? What was she trying to prove? She could go to hell if she wished. Helle fought back, returning fire for fire. Their housemaid ran out of their bungalow and gossiped freely about the quarrel. The wife of the man who lived in the bungalow next to Tunde's remembered all she had seen on TV and cinemas about white women and guns, and feared for Tunde's life.

They reconciled after three days and reached a compromise: they would adopt the baby and then try to have their own.

Tunde named the adopted baby Bimbo. They both agreed that they would not use the name the baby was given at the orphanage.

Bimbo grew up into a plump, well-loved and happy child. Helle loved her deeply. And so did Tunde although, beneath the facade, he still harboured a little displeasure at her adoption. Even after the birth of their own baby three years later, they continued to shower Bimbo with love and affection.

One day in late 1983, Tunde came back from a three-day conference in the eastern part of the country to an empty home. He sat in the living room, furious that neither his wife nor children nor their housemaid was at hand to welcome him. He waited for more than two hours in silence, except for the occasional screams of playing kids outside. At last his eyes caught the brown envelope on the dining table. He reached for it, and found that it was addressed to him. His hand immediately began to shake, as he sensed that something was amiss. Nervously he tore the envelope open. It read:

My dear Tunde,

You will probably be surprised to come back to an empty home. Yes, I asked the housegirl to take one week's leave as soon as you left for that conference. As for our child and I, I am really sorry, but by the time you read this, we will be in Denmark. We will be with my parents for one day and then leave for a place I will not disclose to you because I don't want you to come looking for us.

You may think that I am cruel. Honestly I am not. I left this way because I couldn't tell you my honest feelings, knowing how hard you have worked to make this relationship last this far. The truth is that for the past year or so, I have been feeling terrible. I mean that I suddenly realised that I am a full Dane and can never be happy being a half Dane, which is what our marriage has turned me into. I guess you also became a half Nigerian, and I am not sure that you are happy about it.

You are the father of my kids, so whatever happens, I must make sure that they maintain contact with you. Please take good care of Bimbo and give her all the love she deserves. She may not understand my present action, but please re-assure her of my everlasting love. I do not want to upset you more or interrupt her education by taking her with me.

I will also like to say that even though I don't think that I am still in love with you, you will always remain one of the most loving, caring, and certainly one of the kindest men I have ever met. From the bottom of my heart, I wish you the best of luck in life.

Love,

Helle.

N/B: I have made inquiries about divorce. It is possible for us to get it without being physically present together. At the appropriate time, I will send you the forms. I don't however expect the divorce to prevent you from getting a new wife if you want to, since your culture doesn't oppose polygamy.

At first, he felt it was a cruel joke. It took a while before the reality of it all sank in. He stared at the wall in front of him for some ten minutes, then went to the refrigerator. He found a half-full bottle of dry gin, and caressed it with a little devilish smile. The guttural sounds of his swallow filled the room. Finally, when nothing more would come out, he dropped the bottle on the floor. He thought of sixteen-year-old Bimbo at her boarding school, and felt strangely better. Or perhaps he had merely stopped feeling.

12

The Back-to-God Mission grew faster than any of us had imagined, with the makeshift structure being replaced within one year of the church's foundation. We had a relatively spacious modern building. The structure was dome-shaped and the painting was oily-white. We got the building virtually for nothing, and it happened thus:

One of the regular attendants at our church was an army colonel from the middle belt part of the country. He was a nice man, always smiling. Unless he told you, which he seldom did, you would never know or believe that he was a soldier. I always assumed he was a top banker or belonged to a profession of that nature. Until, that is, the church grapevine got into top gear.

He came to visit me one afternoon, driving up to my home in his weather-beaten Volkswagen beetle car. I saw the car from our window and recognised it immediately. I went out to meet him, as I did with many of our guests.

He was, as usual, smartly dressed. White shirt and black trousers, both neatly ironed. He flashed his customary broad smiles as he saw me. I motioned to him that he was most welcome to our home, and he followed as I led the way inside.

We sat together inside the living room of our three-bedroom home, he at one end of the sofa, me at the other. I couldn't help but wonder why he was visiting, even more so when I noticed that he was struggling for an opening line of conversation. We engaged in small talk, giving glory to God for His wonders and timely interventions. We suddenly stopped talking. The silence lasted for about one long minute. Then he found the courage: there was something he had always meant to tell me, he began, and paused. I did not know what to say so I cracked my voice and said "bless be to the Almighty". This seemed to spur him on, so he began to talk, looking mostly on the floor, but from time to time lifting his face up to meet my gazing eyes.

His story was very touching and he told it in a most remorseful tone: He was an army officer, a colonel, and fought on the federal side during the civil war. One day in 1970, just before the war ended, he was at Aba, commanding the federal troops. They had over-run the city and had captured a number of Biafran soldiers. In the evening they decided to stroll around the village in the hope of finding... well... some women.

I lowered my face to the floor and said nothing. He continued.

In the evening of that day, he was in a room in a deserted compound. The door was locked and she was shouting that she was pregnant, that her husband was around, that her two sons were around.

I didn't ask who the "she" was. He continued his story uninterrupted.

He said he was about to open the door and leave when he suddenly heard furious shouts and banging on the door. His first thought was wether he had survived the battlefields only to be killed by civilians. He didn't think he could accept that so he went for his gun. The banging on the door meanwhile had grown more furious. He thought he heard curses and the screeching of a machete against the cement-plastered floor so he instinctively fired three shots at the door, to frighten them away. There followed shouts of "he has killed our papa, he has killed our papa".

He stopped and looked up at me. Our eyes met. My heart was saddened. But I also knew I had to play cool. He had after all come to confide in me so I mustn't let him down. I went closer to him in the couch and placed my right hand on his shoulder and said, "in the eyes of God, we are all sinners. There is not one of us living in this world without sins, so do not be ashamed of unburdening your soul to the Lord". These words obviously pleased and encouraged him. He tried to look me straight in the face, and to keep his expression blank. I could see that his eyes were getting wet with tears. I fished out my handkerchief from a pocket in my trousers and wiped away his tears. He smiled a dry, funny smile and sobbed. He fished out his own handkerchief, cleared his nose, and continued with his story.

The woman had immediately jumped out of the bed and opened the door. Outside the door was her husband. He was dead, his blood forming a pool around him. Two young boys of about twelve and ten were around the corpse. They were crying and shaking the dead man to see if they could revive him.

As soon as the door opened and they caught sight of him, they left their father and jumped at him, shouting, "you murderer, you killed our father. You murderer, you killed our papa". He tried to fight them off but they were all over him. Suddenly he saw the dead man's wife coming furiously towards him with a machete. He sensed immediately that he had to act fast. He didn't know when he did it. It was an instinctual act, the work of the devil.

He stopped again and looked at me. I managed to keep my face expressionless. I knew from the way he looked at me that he killed the woman and her two sons. I didn't need him to go into such gory details. Somehow he understood this and spared me that. But he said that since that incident, he had never known peace of mind. He had always felt haunted. Almost every night and also whenever he was alone in the daytime, the woman, her husband and their two children would come to dance around him. Usually, they pushed their tongues or pulled their arseholes at him. Sometimes they just jeered.

When he finished his story, he looked at me with deep remorse:

"Pastor, please help me". It was the first time any one had ever called me a "pastor".

After his sad story, I began to think of how to react. After two or three minutes of silence, I suggested that we should go to the prayer house. As we prayed, I began to think of the best possible way to help him. I began praying to God to help me help him, to give me the wisdom He gave Solomon. I closed my eyes and focused on Him. Then I prayed aloud for the next twenty minutes, imploring him to shout, "amen, amen".

The first sentence he uttered when he opened his eyes was "thank you pastor, I already feel better." Less than one month after this meeting, he came back to tell me that the ghosts had stopped appearing. He said he had begun to sleep well, and that he was very much at peace with himself, and with the world. He also began to spread the story that he got healed through me.

He showed his gratitude in kind by way of a Peugeot 504 and a considerable cash donation. Above all, he attracted a number of his friends to the church, and these pooled together their resources to construct a respectable church building. It was, they said, gratitude for what God had done for them through me. Also through his contacts, I began to present a weekly one-hour programme on NTV television, a primetime slot on a Sunday. The church, and myself, was experiencing unprecedented popularity.

13

Madam Cash and Femi quickly settled down in Lagos. Being a very sociable woman, it didn't take her time to establish contacts with the business community, and with the local politicians. Things were moving quite fine for them in spite of the war.

Madam Cash was now popularly called Mama Femi (Femi's mother). She cherished the new name, seeing it as an indication that the bond between her and Femi was cemented. Femi reciprocated this affection.

Madam Cash spoiled the child, who had become a chain smoker by the age of ten. Something of a drunk, he had also become a curious listener to the amorous screeching emanating from Madam Cash's bedroom.

Madam Cash considered herself a very good mother. She felt it was mean to deny kids what adults themselves cherished. Sex was good, she often proclaimed loudly after a good servicing. And believing sincerely in her liberal nature, she had no qualm teaching Femi the mechanics of the game. By the age of twelve, therefore, he knew all there was to know about sex, and was, with the tacit support of Madam Cash, sexually molesting most of the little girls that lived around them.

For a long time Femi and the woman he called mother got along fine. Then, one day, when he was around sixteen, there occurred a watershed in his life. He was in his school where he was notorious for being a bad, bad boy. He had just got up from his siesta. Quite unlike him, he decided to lay back and brood for a while. He was just thinking about what a junior student had the audacity to tell him to his face: the worthiest brain in the most unworthy body. Femi liked the expression.

He got out of his bed and chose to confront the boy again. This time however, behind the facade of a macho boy on a vengeance mission, lay a humbled teenager who was out to court the friendship of a younger one. He caught the sight of the boy as the boy was running up to the classroom to read. He ordered him, with an exaggerated anger in his voice, to stop. The boy turned and stopped still. He knew the rules in this boys-only secondary school: It was run like a military academy with class seniority corresponding roughly to military ranks.

"Kneel down. Why are you getting up from siesta so late?"

The boy knelt down and said nothing.

"You chose to insult me for no just cause this morning. Have I ever done or said anything wrong to you?"

Tears gradually began to stream down the boy's eyes.

"Have I ever said a word to you in this school?" Femi's voice was a little pleading, and a little shaky with pretended displeasure. The boy said nothing.

Femi repeated the question. The boy burst into real tears as he began to answer. He told Femi that he had eight sisters, that he was the only male child of his parents, that he always dreamt of having an elder brother, that he had often spent time imagining how he would love his elder brother to look and act like. He said that he had always seen Femi as this ideal elder brother- big, very intelligent, very courageous but then....

He stopped and lowered his face to the ground. Femi, with his demeanour changing to a friendly one, encouraged him to go on.

"It really makes me sad. I know that someone like you will be a very great man in this world. Why on earth do you want to ruin what you have been destined to be? Why? I can't really understand and it makes me cry many times a week".

Femi can clearly see the love in the boy's face. He asked him to get up and go. He did.

For days, Femi thought about this. It usually stirs up a good feeling in one to know that one is loved and admired, and that one is thought destined for great things.

It didn't take very long for a friendship to develop between Femi and the boy. It started with the boy going to Femi's dormitory every morning to greet him before going for classes. Femi later began to reciprocate those visits. Then it got to a point where the boy began to introduce him as his big brother. Before the school term ended, the boy, without any preaching, had converted Femi into a Jehovah's Witness.

Every one in the school heard about this, and its impact on Femi's behaviour and attitude in life. In the morning assembly one day, the principal even talked about it, and said something about the sky being his limit in this world- if only he could have a modicum of self-discipline.

Femi got home at the end of the school term with the fanaticism of a new convert. Madam Cash came home in the evening and noticed that he was back. She dashed into his room to hug and kiss him as they used to do. She got a very cold rebuff. She was amazed at this passionless reception from him and took time to inquire if she had wronged him in any way. Femi didn't even bother to answer the question.

She asked: "Is it because I didn't come to pick you up in school?" Femi still didn't answer. She dashed out of his room and soon returned with bottles of beer and packets of cigarettes. She hoped to use them to placate him for whatever she might have done wrong. As she placed them on the floor in his room, she said with a little whimsical smile: "I am going to bring a woman for you tonight, the type you have never seen before. I am going to make a very special cele..."

He jumped out of the bed where he was lying in black silence. Kicking away the bottles of beer and the packets of cigarettes on the floor with the fierceness of a roving wild beast, he stammered: "To hell with you! You should be ashamed of yourself!" Then he banged the door, such that the foundation of the building shook, and sent a loud and clear message to her.

That night he fought with one of Madam Cash's teenage lovers who had come to pass the night there. She deliberately decided not to come to the boy's defence. She just sat dumbfounded as the teenage Romeo was humiliated and tongue-lashed. In her mind, theories of why her beloved Femi was suddenly turning against her ran riot. Had she done anything terribly wrong? Had she unknowingly deeply hurt his feelings? Had people been spreading wicked rumours about her?

Throughout the three-week school vacation, Femi hardly said a word to his baffled mother. His hatred for her was only thinly disguised. For her part, she had decided to exercise patience, hoping that Femi would get over it, whatever it was.

Back in school, Femi moved from one extreme form of behaviour to the other. In place of the hard drinking, bragging and noisy 'bad, bad boy', he became a recluse. The only friend he now kept was Dankwa, the junior boy who had unwittingly transformed him. He attended the meetings and prayers of the local chapter of the Jehovah Witnesses regularly but avoided being close to any of the members. He was more devoted to his studies than he ever did, feeling energised by his academic prowess. He became the toast of the school and a form of myth began to develop about him. From this myth-making mill emerged stories of his ferocious appetite for biographies of such men as Fidel Castro, Lenin, Karl Max, Franz Fanon, Kwame Nkrumah, Nnamdi Azikiwe and Abraham Lincoln.

Because of his widely recognised academic ability, every one in the school expected him to read either Medicine or Law. But Femi's mind was entirely his own. He had a different dream of his life's trajectory. And he believed that studying English Literature and Philosophy at the University of Lagos would put him on the course of realising that goal.

***

The relationship between Femi and Madam Cash grew colder as the years went by. She was proud that her son had entered the university but very regretful over the turn their relationship had taken. She had hopes though- a hope that one day Femi would come out of whatever it was that had come over him, and return to his good old self. Each time Femi came to take his school fees, the feeling that his future somehow depended on her benevolence, and that he would one day come to appreciate this, always reinforced her hope. This however turned out to be only a beautiful dream gone sour, for with the passing of each day, Femi got more and more impossible to please.

One day, during the holidays, Femi was in his room, lost as usual in a book he was reading. Suddenly he became aware of a presence in the room. He jumped out of his bed with a start, and was greeted with Madam Cash. "What are you looking for here?" he barked in a tone totally devoid of affection.

"Am I not your mother? Am I not entitled to enter here whenever I like? At least to make sure that everything is alright?"

He kept mute. He was boiling with rage. She drew nearer and saw the book, something to do with revolution and class struggle.

"What is the book about?" she asked innocently and friendly, ignoring the clear message on his face. The question let him loose:

"It is about the historically ordained time when people like you will be swept out of the surface of the earth to make way for a glorious new order. This new era will have no place for people of loose morals- adulterers, capitalists and the bourgeoisie. Man's inhumanity to man must be stopped. Oppression must...."

"You mean you now hate me so much that you...you will like to see me cleaned off the earth?" she stammered angrily.

"That's right", he said calmly. She was shocked and dumb-founded. She stood fixated for a long minute before she furiously staggered back to her room. About ten minutes later, she burst back into the room.

"Listen", she began as calmly as she could, "I think enough is enough. I probably made a mistake. Probably it was my mistake to pick you up where you were abandoned by your heartless mother and gave you a decent life. Now, how do you want to reciprocate my good gesture? To kill me? I won't allow you to do that. By noon tomorrow, I want you to leave this house, and I don't ever want to set my-my eyes on you again". As she stammered out the last sentence, she burst out of the room, giving the door such a ferocious bang that the building vibrated.

***

The following morning Femi packed his belongings. He felt strangely elated. He knew he would be moving from the world of relative security to that of uncertainty. But then, didn't most great men have to go through such a phase? Dankwa was certainly right or rather very prophetic: he was destined to be someone very great.

He felt lucky that he still had a room at the students' hostel. He moved into the room even though the school was still on vacation. He began to think frantically about how to make money. Within one week he had decided to be a part-time motor tout. He had no doubt in his mind that he would one day recount doing the job with a victorious smile.

Femi worked hard at his job. At the same time he never allowed his dream to die. He verbalised much of this dream - or rather his dissatisfaction with the *status quo*, in his creative works. The more dissatisfied he was, the greater his creative and literary output. In no time, he succeeded in selling some of these works to newspapers- a big stride, which for him confirmed the `prophecy' that he had been chosen by history for something great.

School holidays ended about six weeks after Madam Cash threw him out of her home. Femi had enough money to take care of himself. It turned out not to be a big deal combining his work as a tout with his full time studies. He felt actually very happy carrying his destiny in his own hands. This, he believed, had given him sufficient amplitude to figure out his mission in life.

Not long after schools resumed, acute water shortage hit Femi's university. The students were suffering and complaining loudly but the university administration wasn't doing enough to alleviate the situation. Femi felt that a typical revolutionary situation had arisen, and that what the students needed was the right leadership. He chose to provide that by mobilising them for action.

By the time the students were through with their demonstrations, two of the university's buildings were reduced to a heap of ashes. Femi and the other four ringleaders were summarily expelled.

14

Tunde felt cheated. He had done everything to make the marriage work. Yes, he knew from the first time that it would take a lot of compromise and hard work on his part for it to work. And he was determined to put in everything to make it succeed. He very much wanted to make a point- or rather two points. First, he wanted to put to the grave the myth that a marriage between an African man and a white woman was only destined for the rocks. Second, he really loved Helle and wanted to do everything possible to keep her.

No one, not even Helle, would accuse him of not trying. She had complained about his relatives who visited with neither notice nor invitation and yet would stay for days or even weeks and behaved, not as guest, but as if they actually owned their home.

Tunde was decisive about this: he put a stop to uninvited visitors, including his blood brothers and sisters. People from his village who heard about this whistled and gossiped that he was under Helle's spell. A few actually tried to talk him out of such an 'outrageous decision', but he held his ground. His clan ostracised him. His parents and siblings boycotted his home but he didn't give a damn. Helle sympathised with him for his troubles but maintained that she would find it difficult with the idea of his relatives visiting uninvited or without notice.

His mind began to wander: He had had to wait many years before she felt ready to have a child and had accepted much bullshit from her. And now she was gone! Just like the wind. Nonsense! She even had the audacity to coerce him into adopting a baby even before he had his own. Could he have been under her spell? Who said that white people don't make juju?

Tunde was in the room, drunk and feeling bad, when Bimbo, as if by telepathic instigation, walked in from school. She saw him sitting dazed, stupid and helpless on the floor, and immediately knew that something was amiss.

"Where is mummy?" she asked in anxiety, and at the same time gave him a little jerk to rouse him out of his state of stupor. She called Helle 'mummy' and was very much attached to her. She also called Tunde 'daddy', but only because she had to.

He began to cry- loud, like a baby, as he handed her the letter Helle had left behind. She read it with unusual speed, and as soon as she got the crux of the message, she too burst into tears. She cried and cried until she fell asleep on the floor.

She suddenly woke up, alert. No, she wasn't just dreaming. Someone was actually trying to pull her undies. Her blouse was already unbuttoned. She sighed rudely. Anger paralysed her.

This wasn't the first time he had done that. He had done it since she was twelve. He would sneak into her room when Helle was deeply asleep. She never resisted, even though she had always wanted to. So now, as always, she didn't resist, though she felt like strangling him to death. If only she was physically stronger, or had her real parents with her. If only she wasn't afraid. If only...

***

Helle's abrupt departure left a deep wound in Bimbo's emotions. She could not understand why a woman she had all her life known and respected as 'mummy' would decide to leave without her. Wasn't it her who adopted her in the first place? Didn't she show her more affection than she showed even her own children? Could she live alone with Tunde, that monster of a man?

She returned to school after two days of hell with Tunde. From being an extrovert in every positive sense of the word, she became withdrawn, cynical and lonely. At the end of the school term, she swore never to return to Tunde. She chose instead to spend the holidays with a fifty-something-year-old-man, who came into her life by pure chance.

She was standing aimlessly on a road after school that day. Tears were streaming down her cheeks. She was sobbing, daydreaming of running into her real parents. Suddenly a Mercedes saloon car pulled up. The driver had strands of white hair. He seemed cultured, and spoke in a polite manner. Though he was evidently well-off, he put no airs as they conversed. Has God answered her prayers? Can this be her biological father? These thoughts raced in her mind as they spoke.

Soon she found out that the man had three wives. She lied that she didn't have any place to stay because her parents threw her out of their home. The man sympathised and offered to keep her in a hotel. She didn't take long to accept.

He came to see her everyday and always brought a present. He said nice things to her and made her feel loved. She liked that very much, and every day looked forward to his coming. No, she didn't feel that the man was taking advantage of her. Yes, they had sex, but it was only because they were in love with each other. No, the man was not like Tunde. She was sure that he would soon ask her to marry him. What did it matter that he was over fifty and she was just sixteen? Love is, after all, blind. When he asked the inevitable, her inevitable answer would be, 'yes, darling, I will marry you."

The man maintained her in that cheap hotel throughout the three weeks of the school vacation. Her self-esteem received a big boost. Finally, the vacation ended. She was becoming a little lively again. The wound from Helle's departure was beginning to heal.

She expected him to hang around her school everyday waiting or searching for her. This was her second big disappointment in life. The man didn't show up at all for the first two weeks. Then one day, he appeared, telling her tall tales about how some unfortunate developments in his business had left him with no spare time. He said it in such a way that she totally believed him, even sympathised with him.

She didn't see him again after that day. For a long time she believed that there must be a good reason why he hadn't shown up. Then it gradually dawned on her that the man wasn't coming back again. After a couple of other encounters with sugar daddies, she concluded that they were all the same: too nice, for too brief a period. She must never trust them but it was okay to be with them. At least they gave her lots of money and presents as a way of protecting their conscience. That was fine with her. If she could get loads of money and a place to lay her head, she would never wish to see Tunde again. How could he have been so inconsiderate? To have started such a thing with her when she was so young? She recalled the doctor Tunde secretly took her to when, aged thirteen, she had complained of nausea in the morning. She cried at the thought.

Bimbo began prostituting herself each school holiday. Initially, the aim was just to have a place to lay her head away from Tunde. Then she gradually began imbibing the subculture of the oldest profession. Deep inside, however, she hated herself for doing it. She never in her darkest times envisaged such a life. She still yearned to live a straight, uncomplicated life, the way she felt that Helle did. If only Helle had not deserted her....

One day Bimbo was alone in her dormitory thinking over her life. She didn't know her biological father or mother and the pain still hurt badly. She also thought of the moral mess she got herself into and that made the pain worse. Tears were flowing down her cheeks freely. God, she really wanted to be a nice girl. But look at the gap between what she had turned out to be, and what she would really like to be! For some days she was very depressed.

To cleanse her conscience and regain lost moral ground, she decided to join the school's Scripture Union. She felt very happy with her decision. The members called each other 'brother' or 'sister. That was very good for her. She really needed to feel loved. But what would it be like to have real brothers and sisters? This line of thought usually depressed her, so she consciously tried to refrain from pursuing such lines of daydreaming.

Her enthusiasm for the SU began to founder after only three weeks of active membership. What she got from her informal interactions with the members was probably not what she had bargained for. Perhaps she had expected the members to be sort of living saints, much in the same way they acted during their prayer meetings. She was disappointed. She even began to contemplate opting out of the Union completely. She complained loudly that the members' private lives and behaviour sharply contradicted what they preached.

One day, one of the senior members of the Union announced the arrival of an important letter. They were in one of the classrooms having a prayer meeting. It was a Friday evening. Obviously, it was a letter they had been looking forward to receiving. Curiosity gripped most of them. One member suggested that they should say a short prayer before opening the letter. Who knows, their prayer, even at that moment, could change favourably the contents of the letter.

The bespectacled young man who opened the letter involuntary emitted a scream of joy. A spirit of joy suddenly pervaded the room. It was as if the Holy Spirit had suddenly a descended on them. The only significant difference was that, rather than burst into a Babel-like murmur of tongues, hilarious jubilation reigned. What a mighty God they served! Didn't Christ make a solemn promise that "My strength is made manifest in your weakness"?

Bimbo absorbed the news with some indifference: the Union had just received a letter from Lagos. It was a reply to their request for a three -day prayer visit. The request was granted. And more! They were informed that a prominent but undisclosed member of the church in Lagos had undertaken to pay for transport, board and lodging for 25 members. The congregation numbered just 17, meaning that any member who wanted to go was welcome to do so.

She didn't have much to lose by going. After all, the three days they would be away would coincide with a period of public holidays in honour of a certain Muslim feast. Then there was also the fact that she had never been to Lagos before, even though it was just a few kilometres from Ibadan. More importantly, she looked forward to seeing the Back-to-God church. And to listening to Reverend Ogwu, Nigeria's evangelical sensation.

15

Having the opportunity of a regular TV appearance was perhaps the greatest thing that had happened to me. My excitement knew no bounds, though I tried very hard to conceal it under a constant veil of sober ambience. I was exceedingly cautious not to excite anybody's jealousy. Moreover, men of God were expected to look ascetic and sombre.

I was conscious that the Back-to-God church was growing beyond my wildest imagination. I still had great dreams for it. God in His infinite mercy was only beginning to actualise those dreams. The opportunity of regular television appearances was only the beginning of a process. There was no need to despoil this by allowing my excitement to displace the esoteric countenance for which I was known. It would be like the proverbial he-goat who danced himself lame before the actual dancing tournament commenced.

My regular television appearances helped the church's membership to a ten-fold increase. Many of the converts came with effusive praise for the weekly TV programme on family life or, more accurately, for my performances as a televangelist. Whatever I said on the programme usually had strong religious undertones.

One Sunday morning, I went to the church for our usual Sunday service. At the end of the service, I decided to go down to another building, an annex of the church we called 'chapel'. It was a place we went for spiritual retreat or to receive visiting religious groups.

The chapel was in a 150-square-metre ground, about 30 metres south of the church. It was a parlous six-bed-room bungalow, which was always neatly kept. Incense burned there all year round. The aroma of the flowers, coupled with the esoteric perfumes of the incense, imbued the chapel with a divine quality.

Often religious groups would come from afar to this spiritual retreat. This had actually become a big feature of the church, especially since I started those television appearances. We hardly rejected requests for such a visit. Our only proviso was usually that the visiting groups should make their own accommodation and feeding arrangement, though sometimes some affluent members of the church would undertake to shoulder those burdens for some visiting groups. This was seen as part of doing God's work. God would forever reward people who helped others to fortify themselves spiritually.

There were three visiting groups that day. One group was from Jos in the middle belt part of the country, another was from Lagos, while the third was from Ibadan. I spent some minutes chatting with each group and answering the questions they put forward to me.

I took some special interest in the group from Ibadan. This was probably because all the members were teenagers. They said they came from one of Ibadan's secondary schools. This, for me, made the group even more interesting, because it was not often that sec-ondary school students surrendered themselves to a superior power

The students were very interesting. Many of them were versed in the bible. Most had memorised many portions of the Holy Book and seemed all too eager to regurgitate them at the slightest opportunity. They liked using high-sounding English words - the types that filled the mouth. They were full of zeal and very likeable.

They were seven in the group - four boys and three girls. One of the boys asked too many questions about the end-time. Another boy wanted to know more about life after death. One girl asked me my opinion on a marriage between a believer and a non-believer. Another girl asked me what I thought of divorce. The third girl said nothing. She was the only member of the group who did not make a contribution.

*****

I was almost at the doorsteps of my compound when I suddenly realised that someone was racing to catch up with me. It was the girl who did not say anything. She was a member of the group from Ibadan. I was pleasantly surprised that she wanted to talk to me. I had wondered why she chose to keep mum when the other members of her group were literally struggling to be heard or to show off the biblical passages they had memorised. Her face didn't suggest that she was the quiet type. Her expression seemed to suggest that either she didn't like me or that she was disappointed by what she saw.

"Excuse me, pastor", she said in a tiny, shaky voice as she caught up with me.

"Quite excused, my child". I stopped. She walked up to me. She was anywhere between 15 and 18 years old. She was plump with a dark complexion, and seemed to be hiding her natural boldness. She tried to act shy by looking on the ground and drawing patterns with her foot as she talked.

She said she liked my preaching, that she had never

heard anything like that in her life. I thanked her for the compliment and told her that I was glad that she liked it. She paused after this. I knew she was trying to find a way of coming to her main point. I waited patiently for her with an encouraging smile. She found the courage after a while: there was something she would like to discuss with me, would I have the time? I replied to the affirmative, and she smiled. She had a lovely gap between her two upper incisors. She was wearing a nice smelling perfume and appeared happy at my eagerness to listen to her. She asked me when I would have the time for her.

"Do you mind talking now?" I moved on and she followed closely but respectfully behind.

As I opened the door to my lounge, I asked: "My child, what's that your name again?"

"Bimbo". Her voice reminded me of the morning songs of weaverbirds.

16

The world of daydreaming and the real world are two different locations. The one is colourful and rosy and one easily achieves one's dreams through a minor application of will power. The other seems to be lined with thorns and malevolent spirits that stubbornly stand between a man and his dreams.

The simplicity of the dream world was precisely what goaded Femi to create the conditions that led to his being thrown out of Madam Cash's home. It was also what made him view his rustication from the university as part of the divine plan of his inevitable greatness.

The real world was, in contrast to the dream world, rough, tough and nasty. Femi quickly discovered this. He had thought that such a menial job as motor touting would be an all-comers' job. He was wrong. The touts at the Irefe motor park did not take kindly to his appearing from nowhere to come and compete with them and said so to him. He ignored them. He felt that his better mode of dress and superior English gave him an advantage and he was in many ways correct about that. Usually, he stood at the entrance to the park. As soon as he saw anyone who looked like a passenger, he tried to convince him or her to board a particular bus or car. The driver of the commercial car or bus compensated him. This is what motor touting was all about.

On his first day at the job, he had walked up to a young couple travelling to Ibadan. Without much effort, he persuaded them to board a 504 station wagon. The driver of the vehicle gave him a tip for that. Femi frowned. The driver smiled and increased the compensation. Femi's expression relaxed but wasn't showing complete satisfaction. The driver would just have to remember to make it better next time. It was just a deal sealed with eye contact. The driver started the engine while Femi raised his hand in a friendly salute and farewell.

He began to look for other passengers. One's income in this occupation was in direct relation to one's effort.

He was blocked by two sweaty, muscular men who were regular touts in the park. Their grim, fiendish expressions showed clearly that they regarded Femi as an intruder and demanded to know who he was. He knew they weren't asking the question in order to make his acquaintance, so he kept quiet.

"Are you a member of the Union?" one of the men demanded. He had a protruding moustache, stern looks, and very big hands like badly shaped shovels.

Femi regarded him with contempt and turned his face without saying a word. A motor-tout union? He knew that motor touting was not even recognised as a profession. On the contrary, most people regarded them as petty criminals. He knew also that from time to time, the government hounded them. With a supreme will power, he suppressed laughter over the absurdity of the idea.

"You are too proud to answer a simple question". It was a statement rather than a question and it came from the taller of the two men. He was thickset and looked funny in a bowler hat. He had a slight limp in his left leg and seemed to defer a lot to the other man.

Femi still did not answer. He wanted to walk away from them. The thickset man gave him a pugnacious push. Femi got infuriated and retaliated. The man pounced on him. Within a minute, Femi was raised up in the air like a log of wood. He landed on the rocky ground with a thud. Blows rained down. Femi tried to fight back, but was completely overpowered. Blood was oozing out from the sides of his mouth. He was gasping for breath. The other man with the brooding moustache stood by and watched, preventing any intervention. He had a little grin on the left side of his mouth and seemed very content with the way the interloper was being handled. He had two wives and nine children to fend for.

A fat man suddenly appeared from one of the eating sheds at the south end of the park. The confidence on his legs showed that he was someone important in that park. He was wearing a pair of not-so-clean shorts and a sleeveless-shirt. He was about sixty years old, and the longest serving tout in that park.

"Stop that! Will you stop that!" He was barking these orders as he walked towards the scene. The man with the brooding moustache saw him and began to hail him by his alias. At the same time he joined in asking his friend to stop the beating. Femi was out cold, and water was needed to revive him.

After he regained consciousness, the fat man called him aside and blamed him for not following procedure. He was told that, to be *a transport worker* in that park, one must apply in person through him, or be recommended by another member. Femi accepted the blame and apologised, which the big boss accepted. Then he asked Femi to wait while he conferred with four other men. The two men he had quarrelled with were among the four.

He returned to Femi after about ten minutes. He came back with good news: Femi was now permitted to work in the park. There was one proviso though. He had to surrender the tip he got earlier because he worked illegally for it. The arrangement was OK with Femi. He paid the money but was too mentally and physically exhausted to work more that day. The pains from the blows were now beginning to hurt.

He went home. The pains didn't allow him to get up from his bed for three days. On the fourth day, the pains were still there but he needed to make money. He was getting into debt, and the possibility of starvation was creeping in. The alternative would be going back to Madam Cash and asking for forgiveness. He had already sworn that he would rather die than do such a thing. He put on his jeans and baseball cap and looked at his reflection in the mirror. He managed a grin. A strange face grinned back at him. The real world was really nasty and brutish.

***

Working as a motor-tout turned out to be no fun for Femi. It was not because of the nature of the job. He coped quite well and made his daily bread from it. But he was a loner. He didn't get along well with the other workers in the park. No, he had no quarrels with any of them. He was simply disappointed in them. He had sat together a number of times with many of them and had told them of his big dreams for the country, and of the need for a revolution. On each of those occasions, they merely listened very attentively or at least appeared to do so. He had expected them to start looking at him with some respect - as someone who was to go places. They didn't. Femi was disappointed. But he continued in the hope that his colleagues would soon begin to understand about revolution. He only had to work harder to convince them.

One day, one of his colleagues called him childish to his face and he overheard another saying that he was a little on the lazy side. Those gossips killed his spirit. They also made him feel alienated from his colleagues, which in turn made him to detest his working environment.

He made quite some money from being a motor-tout. The job, for sure, would never make him rich. That was not his dream either. It was also not the most respectable job in the world but he didn't give a damn. The most important thing for him was that he got by through that. Soon he managed to save enough money to find himself a room in a dilapidated building in Ajengule, in Lagos.

Many quarters in Lagos would, by international standards, be classified as slums. Ajegunle was one of the worst. It was the ghetto people's ghetto. But it had one thing to its advantage; the cheapest accommodation in Lagos.

The room he moved into was in an unpainted one-story building. There were altogether eleven rooms, five upstairs and six on the ground floor. The landlord had two rooms upstairs with his family. He and his family also had an exclusive use of one of the two sets of toilets and bathrooms in the compound. The tenants in the building numbered over 150. Together they all shared one kitchen, one small pit latrine, and one very narrow bathroom. The latrine was always dirty and stinky and the buzzing sound of houseflies could be heard from a kilometre away. At nights, every available space in the narrow corridor that led to the compound was occupied with mats. Often a number of those mats stank of stale urine. About sixty people slept every night on that narrow, ten-metre long corridor.

Femi liked the place. He believed he would one day

tell the story with pride. He had no doubt in his mind about the course of his destiny. Didn't most great men in history endure such deprivation and humiliation on the road to greatness? He once read somewhere that the hallmark of a man was not that he shouldn't fall, but that he should get up after each fall. Femi was determined. Already he felt that he had recorded some successes: he had through sheer will-power forced the motor-touts at the Irefe motor park to admit him as a worker there, and he had been able to secure his financial independence in spite of odds.

He remembered the time he was a Jehovah's Witness. That was some years ago. He had left the group about nine months after becoming a member after disagreeing with them on what he called 'matters of principle'. Now, he regarded himself as an atheist. But he believed that he learnt one useful lesson as a Jehovah's Witness: the biblical passage in the book of Romans chapter eight, verse 28, which promises that for those who loved Jehovah, all things will eventually work out for good. This passage had been the basis of his constant optimism. In fact, he believed that many laws of nature conformed to it:

Whatever goes up must come down.
After rainfall comes sunshine.
Nothing lasts forever.
No condition is permanent.

Number Nine Ozubulu Street where Femi lived was quite easy to locate in Ajegunle. It stood just opposite the Ukunu Central Hotel. Apart from the hotel, it was the only story building in that area of Ajegunle and it was the area's pride. Its fame rested more on its relative decency. Unlike most other hotels in the area, prostitutes were not allowed to hang around there. It had chalets, but no one was allowed to pay for just one hour's accommodation. In essence, it was priced out of the reach of most of the local guys in the area who needed cheap sex but did not have their own homes or enough money to pay for a full-night hotel accommodation. Many of the hotels in the area had this group of poor young men, often trade apprentices with overflowing libido, as their major clientele. The hotels either offered cheap prostitutes or they offered rooms where one could bring a girl and pay for so many hours.

The Ukunu Central Hotel targeted a different clientele. Its main customers were mainly those who lived outside Ajengule but needed a little decent hideout. The few 'Ajegunlites' who frequented the hotel were mostly those who would be regarded as the upper crust of the area, or who wanted to pretend that they belonged to that class. To have been to the Ukunu Central Hotel for a bottle of beer, was, among the residents of the area, a mark of distinction.

By Lagos standard, Ukunu Central Hotel was neither big nor even decent. It had no air-conditioners and many of its fans were either totally out of order or rickety. It had also no power generator, which meant that, as there were regular power cuts in the country, but more especially in that area, the hotel was often engulfed in a cloud of darkness at nights. But it boasted of many lanterns to its credit. These were kept neat.

There were about eight chalets in the hotel's first floor. The ground floor was a continuous rectangular space and was used as a restaurant and a bar. There were no separate compartments for the bar and for the dining room. Each seat in the long room had its own table (and its own lantern at nights). Compared with the other hotels in the area, the members of staff were as polite as they could be.

Femi's first visit to the hotel was by instinct. He had just moved to the area the day before. The following evening he returned from work to find that the house he lived in was a mass of darkness, thanks to a power cut. He owned neither a lantern nor a candle and was too new in the house to feel comfortable in such darkness.

He stood for a while in front of the house, his mind racing. Where should he go to while away time? He thought hard. Opposite him were streaks of lights from a building. He remembered from the previous day that it was a hotel. He had some money in his pockets, so he decided to go into the hotel and buy himself a bottle of Coca-Cola and read the two newspapers he had with him.

17

I made her feel comfortable in the lounge while I went to my room to undress. My wife came out, and in her characteristic manner, welcomed her very warmly. They sat chatting. From my room, I could faintly hear them. She did the talking while my wife did the listening.

I re-entered the lounge. She was emphasising her point with a little gesticulation of her right hand. I found this interesting for she had kept mum when every other member of her group was trying to impress me.

I sat down and looked from the girl to my wife, hoping to be briefed on the issue under discussion. My wife said nothing. Her eyes were focused on Bimbo. I was not very sure if she was really listening. From the curvature of her lips, however, it seemed as if she was secretly immersed in silent supplications to the Almighty. Bimbo kept talking, revelling in the intrinsic euphoria of having a willing audience. She was saying:

"Actually, I was contemplating quitting the group. I just believed that they were all hypocrites. In the beginning, I was very excited. We called one another brother and sister. This always made me feel wanted and imbued me with a high sense of solidarity with them. As I got to know these so called brothers and sisters better however, I became really very disappointed." She stopped and stole a quick glance at me.

I managed a dry grin and said nothing. I now had a good idea of what she was talking about. I shifted uncomfortably on my seat. A strong wind suddenly began blowing outside. The tall palm trees started some acrobatic displays, itching to impress the passers-by. Some weaverbirds suddenly burst into a long and hilarious laughter, which added a melodious quality to the whining songs of the eastern wind. The aroma of some perfume suddenly filled the lounge. I shifted a second time on my seat. Bimbo cracked her voice and continued.

"But for this trip, I would have formally and informally severed my relationship to the group by now". She shifted her angular position such that she now faced me instead of my wife. She was more herself: bold, proud and even a little arrogant. I cracked my voice and shifted the third time on my seat. She stopped talking. My wife quickly shifted her attention (real or faked) from Bimbo to me. A whiff of air wafted into the lounge and kissed my forehead. I crossed my legs and began to talk. The first three sentences were questions.

"You are obviously not happy with some brothers and sisters?"

"Yes".

"You feel they preach one thing and do another thing?"

"I feel most of them are hypocrites. I hate holier-than-thou morality".

"You are with the group from Gbati secondary school?"

"Yes".

I paused. Neither my wife nor Bimbo said anything. The radio in the kitchen began the four o'clock news. My wife got up, excused herself, and left for the kitchen. Bimbo began this pretension of being a shy one. I began to explain. I told her that the problem was probably from her expectations rather than from the members of her group, and that she should remember that those brothers and sisters she was disappointed in were mere human beings and not saints. I cited many instances from the Bible to show that even the twelve apostles had their fair share of human weaknesses but that Christ, in spite of those weaknesses, still accepted them as His apostles. Light-heartedly, I asked her to remember that she herself was not perfect, and should therefore not expect perfection from others.

She listened attentively while I spoke. I could read from her face and from the humbled movements of her eyebrows that she agreed with my points. She said as much, thanking me for granting her an audience and requested that I should pray for her. She wanted me to pray for her to grow stronger in the faith and for a revelation on how best God would love her to serve Him.

My wife re-entered the lounge as I was about to begin the prayers. She started a hymn, which we all sang with enthusiasm. It was a beautiful hymn and it gave us a great spiritual feeling. While we sang, my mind kept thinking of a relevant passage from the bible. At the middle of our third song, the passage from First Corinthians, chapter 10:14 entered my mind:

No temptation has ever overtaken you that is not common to man. God is faithful, and He will not let you be tempted beyond your strength, but with the temptation, He will also provide the way of escape, that you may be able to endure it.

After the song, I began to adumbrate on the above passage for the benefit of Bimbo. I told her that she must see her long consideration to quit the Scripture Union as a temptation from the devil. "But then our God is a faithful and merciful one", I quickly added with a little grin. "You considered quitting but you never actually quit. I also don't think that it is by accident that we are having this meeting". I paused.

My wife shouted, "Praise God".

I responded, "Hallelujah". Bimbo said nothing. I continued: "The Book of First Corinthians, chapter 10 verse 13 promises that even when God allows us to be tempted, He will also provide us with the way of overcoming or escaping from the temptation. My dear Bimbo, God brought you here to show you the way of overcoming this temptation. Now what is this way for you?"

She lifted up her head, cast a very pious glance at me, and said nothing. My wife began leafing through her bible, searching for a relevant passage. I beat her to it.

"Philippians 4:8", I announced. My wife quickly found the passage and read it out:

...whatever is true, whatever is honourable, whatever is just, whatever is pure, whatever is lovely, whatever is gracious, if there is any excellence, if there is anything worthy of praise, think about these things.

I suggested to Bimbo that she should memorise the passage and should always recall its precepts whenever she felt that any brother or sister was living an unworthy life. She should, I suggested, always look at the bright side of every individual for that was the only way of realising the Christian ideal of universal love.

***

For some inexplicable reasons my wife felt attracted to the young girl. The two sat in the lounge and talked, long after the prayers. I was in my room trying to get a nap. Once in a while, the muffling sound of a guffaw would waffle in my ears. I could recognise when it came from my wife, and when it came from Bimbo.

The next day, the girl came again, this time, on my wife's invitation. I was in the chapel praying with some groups who were visiting us on a prayer retreat. When I came back to my home, my wife told me of the visit, and gave me a summary of their discussion. I didn't feel that the girl needed any special spiritual attention. But my wife did.

She said the girl had a way of suddenly losing concentration during discussions and that she interpreted this to mean that there was something in her past which was too uncomfortable for her, and which she would rather not face. I asked her if she had tried to find out from her what that thing was and she replied in the negative but quickly added: "But she really is a sad girl even though she tries very hard to hide it. For example, after suddenly losing concentration during a discussion, she would burst into a hilarious laughter even though I hadn't said anything funny".

I asked if the girl said anything about her family background. My wife recalled the story Bimbo had told her: Her mother died when she was very young. She was the only child of the mother. Her father's name was Dr. Tunde Johnson. He taught agricultural science at the University of Ibadan. When Bimbo's mother died, Tunde, her father, travelled to Europe and got married to a Danish woman. The woman later deserted him with their kids. No, she doesn't have any problem with her father. They have a wonderful relationship.

My wife said she doubted some of Bimbo's stories and that she felt she had something to hide. She also said that Bimbo was very nervous and evasive each time she asked her (Bimbo) any question about her private life or family. I got confused after my wife told me all these so I just proposed that we should always remember her in our prayers.

We didn't hear again from Bimbo after they returned to Ibadan. Not that we were expecting her to write.

After two or three weeks, we forgot all about her. There were other challenges facing us. Our church was still growing so we had enough to occupy our minds and hands.

Late one evening, there was a knock at the door as we were preparing to go to bed. The person was knocking and shouting, "Please open! Please, pastor, open for me!" The voice was that of a young lady. It sounded tensed and distressed. I went and opened the door. And there she stood!

I found it difficult to recognise her at first. There was a lump on her left eye. The state of her clothes in fact suggested that she had either been involved in a fight or had just been given a severe beating. She looked at least ten years older than the first time I saw her.

"My name is Bimbo, pastor. I have been here before, pastor. I came with the members of the Scripture Union from Gbati Secondary School, Ibadan. You and your wife prayed for me". She said all these almost in one breath. I tried to recall the face. It looked familiar enough. Still, I had my doubts. Appearances can be deceptive, you know.

I opened the door wider and asked her to come in.

My wife remembered her without difficulty. She screamed and asked what happened to her. She tried to talk but burst into sorrowful tears. My wife began to console her. She suggested that I should leave the two alone. I did as she had requested.

She made her take a hot shower and without trying further to find out why she looked the way she did, she made her go to sleep.

Early the following morning, my wife went to her and found out the story. She had not been in good terms with her father since his white wife deserted him. He wanted her to marry his friend whom she didn't like.

He threw her out of his home and stopped paying her school fees because of her refusal. For the past three months, she had been trying to survive on her own. She didn't have money to pay for her school and boarding fees for the coming term. School would resume in only three days' time. She didn't know what to do, and she didn't have a place to stay when school vacated. So she decided to come to Lagos. She was staying at the Good Hope brothel, working as a prostitute. She hated it and herself for doing it but she had no alternative.

Yesterday, at about 8pm, two men came to her cubicle in the hotel. They refused to pay afterwards. She suspected they also wanted to kidnap her for ritual sacrifice so she fought back. Some people came to her rescue. She felt so guilty that she had let herself and God down. She came to us to confess and to see if we could help her in any way.

I felt very touched by the story. There and then I asked my wife if she objected to our taking over paying her school fees, and to harbouring her in our home during school vacations. She agreed readily, and gladly went to relay the good news to her.

18

Femi quickly resigned himself to being a motor-tout. He even began to like the job. He liked the possibility of being constantly in the midst of people, which the job provided. He also derived satisfaction from convincing a passenger to board one vehicle and not the other and even began to relish jokes from his fellow "workers", though not when he was the butt of those jokes. In spite of these however, he didn't allow his dream to die.

Femi didn't have a close friend, and didn't particularly care. His daily programme was the same seven days a week: he left for work before five o'clock each morning, and returned twelve hours later. He usually ate in one of the cheap food kiosks around, and then went to the Ukunu Central Hotel. Normally, he would order a bottle of Coca-Cola and sit as far away as possible from people and write until about eleven o'clock, before leaving for his room.

Initially, he wrote only poems and short stories but none of the magazines and newspapers he sent the stuffs to were interested in publishing them. He remained undaunted. He believed that his works were rejected because the editors clearly recognised his great potential and had, out of jealousy, conspired to prevent him from realising his ambition. This line of reasoning always made him feel good. He felt good in the conviction that there was nothing wrong with his works, and in the conspiracy theory, which he used to rationalise the numerous rejection slips he received.

His first published work was a satire called *The biography of a chicken,* which was published in the prestigious Sunday Times. Here, the usually-stern Femi used a combination of humour and satire to portray the life of a typical Nigerian worker living in Lagos. The work was couched in a Marxist ideological framework. Such works, in those days, appealed to the emotions and compassion of their readers. The satire was obviously well received, for shortly after its publication, a number of newspapers in the country began making references to it. In the next issue of the *Sunday Times,* nearly all the letters to the editor were about the satire.

Femi was of course glad and swore to work even harder. Ten days after the publication of this satire, he was back in the *Sunday Times'* offices. He had under his right arm another hand-written satire, *The wisdom of insanity.*

The literary editor was impressed. He ascertained if he was the same Femi Zed (he chose Zed as his surname when he parted ways with Madam Cash) who wrote *The biography of a chicken* and when Femi affirmed, the literary editor's face began to glow in admiration. He tapped his pen rhythmically on the mahogany table before him, and surreptitiously ran his eyes over Femi, assessing him and his personality. He felt impressed by what he saw and then suggested that they should see the editor-in-chief.

The meeting lasted only fifteen minutes. The editor told Femi that he saw a lot of potential and creative promise in him. Femi immediately remembered a phrase he once read on the blurb of a novel: *a child of great intellectual promise.* He couldn't remember now which novel it was but the fact that the editor-in-chief used a similar sounding phrase to describe him impressed him a lot. He immediately concluded that the editor must be a widely read man, with good literary tastes.

He was offered a full time job as a reporter, which he gladly accepted. And when he was told that the appointment took immediate effect, he very nearly whistled in excitement.

Femi enjoyed the job. He enjoyed hunting for news and saw a lot of similarities between being a reporter and his last job. As a motor tout, he hunted for passengers. As a reporter, he hunted for news. Each had its bright and dark sides: the one was more dignified and more dangerous, the other less dignified and less dangerous.

It didn't take him too long to get himself into trouble. He has been in the job for less than three months. He noticed that each time a big shot called a press conference, envelopes were always distributed to the attending journalists. In the beginning he didn't know what that meant. He had always believed that journalism was the Fourth Estate of the realm and that journalists were the true conscience of the nation. He had, before he became one himself, always admired journalists and writers. He felt that they knew an awful lot, and always admired the strong moral undertones in their writings. He actually used to wonder why the common citizens didn't take to the streets to force the government to hand over power to journalists and writers. After all, they always knew the reasons why things went wrong. They also seemed to have the correct answers for every problem.

One day, Femi was chosen to go and represent the *Sunday Times* in a press conference called by a popular local socialite. One of his colleagues had been visibly angry with the editor for not giving him the assignment. Femi didn't understand why.

At the end of the press conference, envelopes were distributed. Curiosity pushed him to open his own almost as soon as he got it. It contained money. Not much, just a few crispy notes. He was puzzled. What was the money for? He looked at his colleagues in the conference room to see what they did with their own envelopes. None of them made any fuss about it. They simply put theirs in their pockets or bags perfunctorily.

He began to wonder: was the money meant for them to report what the socialite said in the press conference? Or was it meant to make them write a report favourable to him? He felt that, whatever the reason, it was morally wrong of the man to have taken them for a ride, to think that he could purchase them. They were not commodities to be purchased. He was not just angry that the socialite believed he could buy them with money, but also that they could be bought with peanuts.

He tried to discuss this with one of the journalists after the press conference but the man wasn't very interested in the topic and dismissed him with a wave of the hand, saying something about having a wife and two kids to feed. When Femi tried to push the discussion further, the man, with only a thinly veiled disgust, said something of not being interested in having arguments with idealists and Marxists. Femi swallowed hard and resolved there and then to discuss this with his editor.

His editor said such things were not morally proper but the way he said it didn't quite satisfy him. Femi suggested that he should write a critical article about it but the editor was against the idea, arguing that whether a journalist accepted an envelope or not was a moral decision, which only the journalist involved could make. Femi didn't agree. He went ahead and wrote an article on it. The editor refused to publish it.

He sent it to a left-leaning local tabloid known for its radicalism, which eagerly accepted it.

The article mentioned the socialite by name and it became a big scandal. The socialite was not amused and began to throw his weight around. He called the editor of the tabloid that published the piece and threatened terrible things. He did not mince words: he would make sure that the paper was put out of circulation. He said that he could do this by instituting a multimillion Naira libel suit against the paper and using his connections to ensure that he emerged victorious; or he would simply pull certain strings at high governmental levels and the paper would be banned.

The socialite felt kind enough to give the paper an alternative: it could retract its story and issue an apology. The retraction and the apology should be printed on the paper's front page, and should run for seven consecutive days. The editor of the paper knew that the socialite wasn't bluffing and nervously obliged.

At the Sunday Times office, the editor was furious with Femi and summoned him to his office shortly after the publication of the piece. Brandishing the article before him, he demanded to know why Femi chose to publish it against his advice. Femi's defence was an ideological treatise on the moral obligations of a true journalist. He argued, in a rather pedagogic manner, that a politically conscious journalist owed it to the society to expose the various strategies used by the bourgeoisie to maintain their control over the common people. "Can't you see, editor, that the issue at stake here is power? By inducing journalists to portray him and his speech in a very good light, he is hoping to enhance his power and prestige over the masses. What he did amounted to using the media for his own personal aggrandisement".

The editor was furious. He neither had the time for

his ideological big talks nor for mellifluous phrases. He wanted straight answers and nothing more. He would be the last person to accommodate acts of insubordination. He had constantly been receiving complaints from the other reporters and writers that Femi was very difficult to work with. A constant accusation was that he was always set in his ways, and had difficulties in observing simple instructions from his superiors.

The editor had called him two or three times to defend himself against those allegations. Each time he let him go free with only a half-hearted admonishment to be a team rather than a solo player. Privately, he felt the other journalists were only being jealous of him. He knew that Femi was a good reporter, and even better as a writer. Though the editor usually advised his writers to avoid using big words, he always found something thrilling and poetic about Femi's writings, in spite of his penchant for big words and flowery phrases. The editor also secretly admired Femi's reputation for having a seemingly endless repertoire of topical quotable quotes.

That day however, the editor was not in the mood to give any admiration. If anything, he was quick to notice that Femi had used the phrase 'personal aggrandisement' more than three times within the ten minutes that he had been in his office. He felt that that alone made nonsense of his reputation as a good speaker.

Anger was still welling up in him for being slighted by Femi. He was struggling to keep cool as Femi defended himself in the most irritating manner. Suddenly the telephone rang. Femi instinctively stopped speaking. The editor picked up the receiver with a slightly shaky hand. The man at the other end of the line was probably a big shot because the editor kept answering, "yes sir, yes sir". Femi, unruffled and sitting opposite the editor, felt that his boss trembled each time the voice at the other end said something. He also felt that for each sentence the voice uttered, his boss answered "yes sir" twice.

Finally, the man at the other end stopped talking. The editor put the receiver down with a deliberately measured calmness. He locked the fingers of his right hand against those of the left and began to bite his lower lip in a suppressed anger, nodding his head as he did so. After about one long minute, he unlocked the fingers, briefly closed his eyes and quickly ran his left palm against his face.

Femi sensed that the editor was battling to suppress a boiling rage. He said nothing and felt that he had all the time in the world to wait for his boss to exhaust himself with his psychological game. It took another long minute before the editor said: "You have been here less than three months but you have done more than anyone here to bring us to disrepute. I want you to explain in no more than three sentences why you should not be fired with immediate effect". His voice was very combative, yet menacingly calm. Femi had never seen him so annoyed. He thought of how to defend himself, or rather how to justify what he did. He had no iota of doubt that what he did was the right thing to do.

He was not afraid of being sacked. On the contrary, as soon as his boss made it clear that his job was on the line unless he could immediately come up with an acceptable excuse or apology, he began to romanticise the idea of being martyred. He started to visualise all the papers in the country carrying his photograph and the story of his sack 'for being an anti-corruption crusader' He even started to think of how famous he would be in the country's universities, especially among young social science students. These lines of daydreaming made him resolve that he would neither apologise nor recant what he wrote. Some passages he memorised immediately dropped into his mind and seemed apt under the situation.

"Well", he began. "I know that what I wrote would not make me popular either with the powers that be or with most of our colleagues. But I did that in the service of truth. In doing that, I was inspired by the revolutionary words of Frantz Fanon in his message to the youths of Africa. With your permission I quote". He paused to see if he had the permission of his boss to make the quotation or not. The editor was simply too angry to say anything. Femi deliberately chose to interpret his silence to mean acquiescence. He began the regurgitation: *The future will have no pity on those who, possessing exceptional ability of being able to speak the words of truth to the oppressors, have instead taken an attitude of cold indifference and passive complicity.*

He looked at the editor to see his reaction and it was clear he was not impressed.

"You didn't even make a correct quotation of what Fanon said". His voice was loaded with a mixture of anger and disgust.

"Well, quoting him very correctly isn't that important. The most important thing is passing across the kernel of his message".

"You should watch your tongue and mind how you talk to me." It was an order rather than an appeal. Femi understood it as such but refused to be cowed.

"I have a lot of respect for you, boss. I know you mean well and that you want the best for the Sunday Times...."

"Please, don't patronise me".

He continued. "In a situation like this, I always remember the immortal words of Theodore Roosevelt.

With your permission I quote again: *The best executive is the one who has sense enough to pick good men to do what he wants done, and self-restraint enough to keep from meddling with them while they do it.*

"I have heard enough of your stupid quotations. You are sacked with immediate effect. Goodbye and good luck".

"You can't sack me without giving me a month's notice". Femi didn't know when he said this. He just recalled that it was embodied in his letter of appointment. Instinctively he got up from his seat. He didn't want to be taken unawares by anyone or anything.

The editor swallowed hard and aggressively tore out a sheet of paper. As he began to write he said, "You will take this to the accountant and be paid one month's salary in lieu of notice. After that, I don't ever want to see you around here".

Femi stood for a while and watched his bile-filled boss. He too was boiling. For a while he thought of seizing the paper from him, and giving him a bit of the sharp tongue he had learnt in his days as a motor-tout, but quickly decided against it. After about a minute or so of trembling with anger - not for being sacked, but for what he regarded as the hypocrisy of his boss, he blurted, "to hell". As he left the office, he banged the door so hard that some mosquitoes at the corners of the ceiling in the room got rattled.

At his desk, he quickly gathered his belongings, and without saying a word to any of his colleagues, he left the building. As he trotted to the bus stop, his mind was neither on the harmattan wind that was forcibly kissing his lips, nor the man laced with a car tyre and set ablaze by angry traders for ostensibly stealing a packet of salt. Rather, he was concerned about how history would judge what he did.

19

When the school term ended, Bimbo came to spend the holidays with us. My wife had taken the time to write her some letters, encouraging her to do her best in her studies, and assuring her of God's abiding love. She always replied duly. Sometimes the tone of her letter was excessively polite, sometimes melancholic, sometimes too boisterous, sometimes too religious, but at all times grateful. She wrote almost every week, sometimes twice a week. My wife wrote to her every fortnight. I only wrote to her once, no more than ten sentences. Basically, my letter was meant to strengthen her faith in the Lord, and to encourage her not to be a captive of her inglorious past.

She was quite happy to be with us and told us so herself. Before long she began calling my wife "auntie". Me, she called "uncle". Neither my wife nor I questioned this. We knew she didn't mean any harm.

Agada, my first child, came back a couple of days after Bimbo moved to stay with us. He was now a young man of almost twenty-four, and nearly six-foot tall. He had just completed his bachelor's degree in African History, and had been pressurising me to send him to London to read Law. I always told him that I didn't have the money for that, and that even if I did, I didn't think it was a good idea to send him out of the country. I suggested that he should remain in the country as a way of demonstrating his solidarity with the masses of our people. He didn't buy the idea, arguing that travelling out of the country would open his eyes to new possibilities, and that that would put him in a better position to fight for the poor. We always disagreed on this but we were lucky that the disagreement didn't affect our close relationship. It was true that he refused to be enthusiastic about the Back-to-God church but I didn't think that our disagreement had anything to do with it.

During his latest visit, he kept stealing glances at Bimbo. She sensed this and immediately put on the shy act. I introduced Bimbo as our sister in Christ, and announced that she would be staying with us during the holidays. Agada chose to stay with us longer than he normally did.

One day, I returned from our mass service, a little exhausted. I was shuffling to my room to take off my cassock. Suddenly, I noticed that the door to Bimbo's room was slightly open. Instinctively, I decided to peep in and make sure she was all right. She wasn't. She was lying on the bare floor and reeling under the pool of her tears. I was taken aback. "My God" unconsciously escaped from my mouth. I quickly recollected myself, quietly entered the room, and shut the door.

"What's wrong, Bimbo?"

She was oblivious to my presence. Her sobs had the sounds of a dying ember.

I began to give her some affectionate shakes and encouraged her to get up and lie on the bed. She resisted for a while but then allowed me to help her to the bed. I used my bare hands to wipe away her tears. She sneezed while I did this and some mucus fell onto my hands. They had the soft feelings of early morning dew. I wasn't too quick to wipe it off. It was important for her to know that I cared.

She told me later why she felt so depressed: she had recalled a number of things in her life and they made her feel too uncomfortable. The man she told me was her father was not actually her biological father, only her stepfather. She didn't know who her real dad was and no one had told her anything about him. She also didn't know who her real biological mother was. Helle, her stepmother, never brought up the topic for discussion andd she never asked. Her stepmother was really nice to her but her stepfather was a shit of a man.

She was shocked and very disappointed that Helle left for her country without telling her. Given the way Helle cared for her, she could still not believe that she had the heart to treat her so cruelly. Sometimes she would wonder if she had disappointed her, or wronged her in some way.

Since her stepmother left the country some four years ago, she has written her only three letters and never wrote her address in any of those letters, which meant that she couldn't write her back. The last letter she got from her was just two days before the end of the school term. She wrote among other things that she had moved in to live with a man named Søren.

She was quite a happy girl when Helle was living with Tunde. She had a feeling that Tunde, her stepfather, never liked her. In fact, Helle once confided in her that Tunde initially opposed her adoption. Tunde was not really a nice man. Many times when they were still living together, he would sneak into her room. He always did that when Helle was deeply asleep but she never had the courage to stop him from pulling off her clothes each time. She also never had the courage to tell Helle. Might be this was why she left for her country. Might be she found out and got angry with both of them. But it was wrong of her to leave the way she did.

It was also wrong of her not to want a child she adopted to write to her. She would never trust any white woman again.

It was after this that she started living a bad life. Initially, she started following men in order to avoid returning to her stepfather. She really hated him and would kill him if she had the chance. He made her go bad.

She repented and turned to God but something always kept her from living as morally upright as she wanted. When my wife and I came with our offer to pay her school fees, and for her to stay with us each holiday, she felt she had bid final farewell to bad living. But then two days before the end of the term, on the day that she received Helle's letter, she was really feeling so down that she felt she needed a shoulder to lean on. So she put on her wig and went to a local hotel at Ibadan and prostituted herself. She couldn't believe that she did it again. She felt like taking her life.

She felt better after this confession. She had stopped sobbing, and was sitting on the bed. Her face was lowered to the ground as if waiting for my judgement after the confession.

I said nothing for a long while. She too said nothing. It was a noisy silence that was rhythmically pierced by the loudness of our breathings. At last, I found my voice.

"Don't worry. Our God is a most merciful Father. I am sure He has forgiven you. I believe that by feeling bad about these deeds, and by crying and confessing them, you have already done the penance for those sins. Doesn't the bible tell us that the 'sacrifices acceptable to God are a broken and a contrite heart?' Rejoice therefore and sin no more".

My voice didn't have its characteristic force of conviction. My mind was beginning to entertain some sinful thoughts. It was beginning to imagine Bimbo in her prostitutes' bunk selling her ware to her customers. Quickly, it shifted to thoughts of what possibly transpired between her and Agada when he visited the last time. Then it shifted back to her and her stepfather. I could, with my mind's eyes, see her under the weight of Tunde's muscles during the silent tranquillity of dark nights. My mind immediately shifted back to her and my son, Agada. Did they really do it? Was it in her bedroom or in Agada's? Unconsciously, a question escaped from my mouth:

"Did you... with Agada?"

She shook her head in the negative. She seemed to read my thoughts. I looked at her. Her blouse was hanging very loosely on her shoulders, revealing her left breast. It looked full and ripe. A still small voice suddenly began drumming into my ears: if your right eye causes you to sin, pluck it out and throw it away...

I stood up immediately, patted her paternally on the right shoulder, and left for my room to pray.

***

Her confessions brought us closer. I chose not to tell my wife about those confessions. It was probably the first time since I gave myself to the Lord that I kept some secrets from her.

We were soon very conscious of the presence of each other. She suddenly began avoiding the lounge each time I was there, or quickened her pace whenever our paths crossed. On my own part, I began thinking of her during our nightly prayers. During the following Sunday service, I noticed that she hid herself behind a big woman. I suspected that she did that just to avoid any form of eye contact with me. For the first time since the foundation of the Back-to-God church, I felt distracted during a service.

At the end of that service, I went to my room to pray. I was asking God to cast away the spirit of distraction and temptation from me. I was praying Him to make a revelation about Bimbo to me: was she someone in serious need of my assistance? Or was she just sent down by the devil to try and confuse me? I was also praying Him to reveal to me the reasons for this my new-found attraction to her: Was there an obscene motive behind it? Or was it just based on innocent sympathy?

I made three big resolutions about her even before I finished praying:

I would henceforth stop being unnecessarily conscious of her presence.

I would still show her all the affection and love she needed but I would never allow myself to be led into sin from trying to be nice to her.

I held tenaciously to these resolutions until she went back to school. I received two nice letters from her shortly afterwards. In them, she said that her five weeks' stay with us had changed her life for the better. I replied, encouraging her to work harder in her studies, and to allow God to take charge of her life. My wife also wrote her many letters. In each letter, she always let her know that we missed her company and always encouraged her to entrust her life in the unshakeable hands of God.

She came back to us after fifteen weeks. Schools were once again on vacation. After the vacation, she would have only one more school term to complete her secondary education. In our home, she began to float the idea of going to the university to study English Literature. I always told her it was a brilliant idea.

Later, I began to help her with her studies. As a former teacher, I enjoyed this because it was a wonderful feeling re-living that period of my life. I liked helping her in her studies for another reason: the innate human craving to be a big part of success.

Everything was going very well in the beginning. I either went to her room or we would stay in the lounge. Usually, I helped her for about one hour at a stretch. My wife was happy that I found the time to do that. Obscene thoughts never crossed my mind during those periods. I had successfully cast away the tempting spirit of lascivious thoughts.

I was in her room one evening. My aim was to see how far she had gone with the assignment I gave her two days before. My wife wasn't home. She had travelled down to our village to visit her ailing parents. She was to be away for two days.

She was lying face-downwards on her bed and was wearing a nightgown, which was white and transparent. The light, which she had left on, made it possible for me to see the rising and falling of her back as she breathed. The movements lacked rhythm. I suspected that something was wrong, that she was probably crying. I sat beside her on the bed, and began to inquire what was amiss. I quickly noticed that she was lying in a pool of her tears.

"What's wrong, Bimbo?"

Sobs. Long sniffs of the nose. A quick clearing of her eyes with the back of her left hand. A bout of suppressed crying. Head back to the pool of tears.

I persuaded her to stop crying and to unburden herself to me. I helped her to sit up straight. "What is it again, Bimbo?" She wanted to say something but found herself overwhelmed by the weight of sorrow. She dropped herself, from chest upward, on my laps, and began to cry.

After a while, I felt something so soft that certain thrills began circulating in my spines. Those obscene thoughts immediately began playing drums in my mind. My eyes looked down at the back torso of Bimbo as it heaved up and down. Guitarists and percussionists joined the drummers in my mind. My blood became warmer and warmer and warmer. She suddenly looked like the most perfectly sculptured creature I ever saw. I swallowed hard. Suddenly I acquired a satanic intelligence: first, I started stroking her back, pretending that it was all part of the scheme of helping her out of her doldrums. Then I began wiping away her tears with the back of my hands. Then I started kissing the tears on her eyes, reminding her as I did this, that God loved her and that she could absolutely rely on me as a friend, father and pastor. I noticed that she suddenly became conscious of my kissing her. I stopped.

"Now, will you tell me why you are feeling so bad? Remember that I care a lot". There was a pause. Then she said that she didn't know why she was feeling bad. I asked her if it had anything to do with guilty conscience and she answered that she didn't think so. After a long interval of silence, I asked her if she had had any form of sexual activity since making her confessions. Her eyes got watery with tears. Then the tears began streaming down her cheeks.

The Satan in me became activated. Ideas began running riot in my mind. One of those ideas quickly gained dominance over the others. I asked, "Do you want me to pray for you and cast away forever this spirit of fornication".

She nodded her head in the positive. I quickly moved to the door, and assuring myself that no one was in the lounge, I locked the door. I moved to her, and fastidiously began pulling off her clothes. As I did this, I was at the same time shouting very loudly: "I command you evil spirits and principalities to leave this body forever. I cast you away in the mighty name of Jesus. This body is the temple of our Lord. Therefore I command you to get out of here and stop despoiling this temple".

She seemed quite surprised that I was pulling off her clothes but she did not resist. With her clothes off, I began running my right hand over her lower abdomen. At the same time, I began praying more loudly - mostly in tongues. Her eyes were closed, initially out of respect to God, but after a while, for other reasons. She offered no resistance when I pulled her legs apart. In less than ten minutes, it was all over.

After this, I became overwhelmed by guilty feelings. I apologised to her many times. I also secured her word that no other ear would hear of it. In return, I gave her lots of money. I also promised her that I would pick up the bill if she secured admission to the university. I had never felt so remorseful in my life. I vowed to myself never to do that again. But less than twenty-four hours after that, she lured me into doing it again with her.

My wife finally returned from her visit to our home village. I told Bimbo it was over, that we couldn't continue that game. She didn't want to help matters. She probably didn't want to lose her steady source of income.

One Sunday, I was in the lounge with my wife. Suddenly, Bimbo was standing before us. It was only five days before the resumption of school. I was secretly panicked: Had she come to spill the beans?

She asked in a most respectful tone if we could pray for her in the chapel. She said that she wasn't feeling well, and that she badly needed God's intervention. My wife was excited at the request. I was relieved. Bimbo led the way to the chapel. There, I asked her to kneel down in prayers. My wife was standing beside me, with her eyes closed, and hands spread out in prayers. My eyes were also closed. I began to pray. I have hardly prayed for two minutes when I felt a tapping on my leg. I opened my eyes. Bimbo's eyes were wide open. She had a piece of paper, which she quickly handed over to me. Like a clever thief, I took the paper fast and put it into my pocket. I looked at my wife. Her eyes were still closed and she was praying in tongues. I closed my eyes and joined in.

***

When I got to my room, I locked the door and fished out the piece of paper from Bimbo. It read:

Please can you meet me at the Ukunu Central Hotel, Ajengule, It's opposite no. 9 Ozubulu Street. It is very important. Meet me between 1&2 PM tomorrow. I will leave here by 9 am tomorrow for the library. From there I will go to the hotel. It is a nice and safe place.

    Love.

I was very confused after reading this. How could she expect me to come and meet her at a hotel? Didn't she know that some people there might recognise me? I was very angry and at the same time very nervous. Had she become pregnant? If I didn't go, would she blackmail me? I became very afraid. By the following morning, I had caught fever. It was the first time in years that I had been ill. What to do? After many hours of uncomfortable thinking, I concluded that the consequences of not going would be more unpalatable than the effects of meeting her.

By one o'clock the following afternoon, I left for Ajengule. On the way, I stopped at the Ojuelegba market and bought a baseball cap, a big American-type sweatshirt, and a false beard. I went to one of the public toilets in the market and changed. I looked at myself at an old dirty mirror on the wall and felt satisfied at what I saw.

She was standing at the entrance to the hotel when I arrived. She didn't recognise me at all. But as soon as she did so, she asked me to follow her upstairs. She had already booked a room in the hotel.

The hotel was neat, and there were only a few customers at that time of the day. Somehow my nervousness began to ease once we got into the room. I went straight to the point: "Why do you want to see me here? Don't you know that people may recognise me?"

She gave a sardonic smile. "Here is safe. I don't think anyone will recognise you here. Especially the way you are dressed. It's funny, but cute". Her confidence as she said this reminds me of the confidence I normally exuded on the pulpit. She obviously knew this branch of life much more than I did- at least since I gave my life to God.

I returned to my question: "So why do you want to see me, Bimbo?" My voice was now mellifluous. Hers was honey: "I have realised that I love you. I want to be with you. Is it a bad thing?"

I was confused. I knew it wasn't right that this should continue. I was too weak, too full of sympathy, or too afraid to resist. When she began pulling off my clothes, I put up no resistance.

We agreed to meet again at the same place in two weeks' time.

20

My affair with Bimbo blossomed. In the beginning, I was an unwilling participant, but after a while I became fully part of the fun. My conscience no longer disturbed me, and I began to look forward to the meetings.

Bimbo was almost crazy about the affair. For her, it was just more than a question of money or promises to pay her fees. I suspected that the fact of conquering a television celebrity must have been satisfying to her. Moreover, unlike the other married men she had been with, I was always honest with her. Each time we made an appointment, I always turned up. Each time I made any promise to her, I made sure I kept it. I must admit that she was also always honest with me. Not once did she fail to turn up. Not once did I send a message to her through our normal channel without her responding promptly to my wishes. Therefore, with time we became not Romeo and Juliet, but David and Jonathan. Our affair was strengthened by the bond we had made at the heat of passion: we must remain faithful to each other, and must never allow a third party to know of the relationship.

Ukunu Central Hotel was our love-nest. We met regularly there. I decided to make a one-year deposit for one suite. The idea was to minimise the risk of being recognised. I always came to the hotel in my baseball cap, and wearing the false beard. Each time I showed up, I always knew which room to walk to. I didn't even need to acknowledge the receptionists since there was always a chance that a very observant person might recognise my voice, and I didn't want to take any chances. I also loved the solemn assurance from Bimbo that she would keep her lips tight about the whole thing. I trusted her.

One day, in July 1988 after Bimbo had finished her secondary education and had, through my help, secured a job as an office assistant in a private company, I called to tell her that I would like to see her at the usual place. Using our special code, I told her the time I would be there.

I guess she already had an idea why I wanted us to meet. She still lived with us, and was aware that I had just been awarded an honorary doctorate degree in theology by a university in America. The awarding university existed only on the elaborate certificate, of course, which had cost a lot of money.

There were two reasons for this acquisition. First, I believed that it would bestow some academic aura on the church and me. Evangelical churches were springing up at every corner of the country, and those churches whose leaders had academic titles seemed to be more respected. Second, I felt it would make a good impression on my wife and on Bimbo. I knew Bimbo was crazy about people with academic titles. I felt that once I got mine, I would be very close to meeting all her male expectations. Similarly, I believed that such a title would earn an even deeper love from my wife since it was increasingly becoming a mark of elitism in our country to have academic titles. I simply didn't want to be left behind.

The award given to me had a very nice citation:

For your astuteness in founding and nurturing the Back-to-God church; for your invaluable contributions to the course of God's Holy Kingdom through your sermons and counselling; for your inestimable contributions in putting peace and the love of God in many homes in your country through your weekly television programme; and for your consistency in practising what you preach; the Dandy Christian University at New York confers on you an honorary doctoral degree in theology.

Congratulations Reverend (Dr.) Pete Ogwu. May you and your family remain blessed.

My wife's displeasure disappointed me and meant that we wouldn't celebrate the award. But I was thrilled and excited and determined to accept the award. And I knew Bimbo would be happy to share this wonderful moment in my life.

***

Bimbo called my wife from her office shortly after I called her. She lied to her that one of her friends was ill and that she would be visiting the friend after work. She said she would go straight from the office, and might spend the night with the friend. As usual, my wife didn't object. She was not a suspicious person by nature.

Bimbo got there by around four o'clock. Our appointment was at seven. She arrived with two of her colleagues. I guess she was with them just to show off, to force them to respect her by letting them know she got invited to such opulent hotels.

On arrival, she took them to our love-nest at suite number 17. This was against my agreement with her. The three stayed there for a while. Suddenly, she realised what she was doing and took them to the bar.

She was unusually haughty that day. Like a sixteenth

century princess, she ordered three plates of rice and three bottles of beer, billing them to my account. That was our agreement.

At a far corner of that rectangular space that served both as a bar and a dining room sat a serious-looking, square-shouldered young man. He had the kind of full beard that reminded one of orthodox Marxist revolutionaries. He was wearing a worn-out short-sleeve shirt that was indecently buttoned, displaying his hairy chest. A bottle of Coke sat before him. Pieces of paper and a couple of magazines ran riot on the table. The young man was busy writing and didn't even notice the three girls who sat around the table next to his until they began to behave in an animalistic fashion.

As the pitch of their babbling continued to soar higher and higher, the young man was forced to look at them in a manner that politely suggested that they should lower their voices. They ignored him. The young man refocused his attention on his writing, believing that he had made his point, and that the young girls would be reasonable. After about five minutes, he was forced again to look sharply at them. This time around, his eyes wore no polite colours. The message in them was as clear as *Iyegboma* spring water: they should shut their mandibles on their own or they should be sealed for them. The girls dabbled into a hilarious laughter, and kicked their legs as they amused themselves at the expense of the young writer.

"Hi, man, do you think this is a library? You gotta be nuts", declared one of the girls, trying to make her English sound Cockney. The other of the two girls with Bimbo also taunted the young man.

"The Achebes and the Soyinkas wrote their books in their homes or in the libraries. What do you think you are doing here? You're just deceiving yourself. You better go and find yourself a job instead of hanging around here pretending to be writing. What are you writing about, lazy man".

Bimbo wrapped up the ridiculing: "I have seen him here a number of times. I know he is mad. What surprises me is why they should allow a man like this to be around here. He stinks like an Ajegunle gutter. That's why this place is deserted. I will make sure that he is stopped from coming here or I will stop patronising this place".

***

At around seven o'clock, when the two girls had left, I walked straight to suite number 17 and tapped gently on the door. A smiling Bimbo welcomed me with a hug. She was wearing only her undies. I gently locked the door, pulled off my false beard, and drew her to the bed.

21

One evening, Bimbo was at the Ukunu Central Hotel to meet me at seven o'clock in the evening, as agreed. As was usual with her, she was there much earlier than the appointed time. She waited until about half past six and, when there was still no sign of me, she was driven by boredom into the hotel's bar.

***

At the bar, a full-bearded young man was sitting at a far corner. A bottle of Coca-Cola was on his table. He was sitting alone, writing, and was oblivious of the presence of the five or so persons sitting not very far from him, and discussing in low tones. There were a couple of lines on his forehead, which spoke volumes about the level of his concentration. Once in a while a smile emerged. Sometimes the muscles of his chin tightened in obvious sadness. No one in that bar knew what he was writing about. The barman had seen some of his published work and was very proud that he knew him. The barman kept one of the young man's satires, which was published by the Daily Times. "That guy is a genius. He is a Chinua Achebe or Wole Soyinka in the making", he would say. The unfortunate thing however was that only a few people asked questions about the young man. Even those who did, and were shown the young man's published works, always asked how much he made from them. And their faces hardly ever showed that the published works they were shown had increased their respect for him.

Bimbo had no difficulty in recognising him.

She bought a bottle of cola and moved to the bar section of the hotel. As she came close to where the young man was sitting, he raised his head. She missed her step and froze for two long seconds: should she sit beside the young man they had berated, insulted and harassed two weeks before? Or should she move out of trouble's way by finding another seat and pretending not to have recognised him?. She tried to read the expression on his face. She didn't read any anger. But she couldn't swear she was right in her assessment. Suddenly, the left side of his face broke into a half smile. She smiled back, showing her full dentition.

"Can I sit here?" She meant the chair directly opposite him. She didn't know when the question escaped from her mouth.

"Feel free", he replied with a smile.

The young man stopped his writing and laid down his pen. A discussion quickly developed. Bimbo began with very effusive apologies. She said she was deeply sorry for what had happened the last time; that it was all the work of the devil, and that she was still feeling guilty from the incident. The young man told her not to think of the incident, and not to feel bad.

"You mean you have really forgotten? Or you are just trying to be nice?" He was surprised at her directness and immediately concluded that she must be an honest person. He allowed thirty long seconds to pass before he answered: "Well, I do not like being mired in the past. For one thing, such an attitude to life gives frequent mental illness. Besides, the past can never be relived". He said these slowly and deliberately, giving the impression of a very prudent speaker.

Bimbo was instantly impressed. "Is that a quotation from someone?"

His ego was massaged and he liked it. He smiled that half-face smile, and shook his head in the negative. "I said it just now. Does it sound like a quotable quote?"

"Yes".

"Well, it is not".

"I like the sound of it".

"Thank you".

Two minutes of silence that seemed like eternity.

"Can I see what you are writing?" The young man hesitated and then shook his head. "It's not that I don't want you to read it but it is still in the process of being created. If I give it to you to read, I risk losing the push necessary to complete it. It's almost like taking the quiver off one's arrows".

She looked disappointed.

"What's the title?"

"Well, the tentative choice is *When the gods fart*."

She became more curious. "It's a very strange title. Can't you tell me what it is about? I mean just the theme".

That half-face smile hovered again on his left face. "Please understand. Ok, I'll give you one of my published works. I also promise that once this is finished and published, I will give you a copy. What I am writing now is a satire, but what I will give you is a poem. Do you like poems?"

She answered: "Yes. I hope to study English Literature in the university".

He cast an affectionate glance at her and handed her the poem, published in the *Lagos Echo*. It read:

SONGS OF A PRODIGAL

The Christmas bells are ringing.
Everyone I know talks of going home.
Me, the talk is continuing my odyssey.
Before the echo of empty streets swallows me,
as everyone lives for their villages.
I am a self-conscious prodigal,
on a society-imposed exile.
Where is my home?
And who are my friends and siblings?
Their faces and names keep changing,
as I continue my odyssey into the unknown.
Sometimes my soul yearns for some permanence,
if only to laugh longer with the friends I make,
and learn their middle names and surnames.
But such, I guess, is the way of prodigals.
So tomorrow I must again keep my date with Destiny,
while praying that my soul may know some permanence,
before the arrival of my apocalypse.
By: Femi Zed

She read the poem once, twice, three times, silently. Then she lifted up her face. It had suddenly become clouded. He knew that the melancholic tone of the poem had overwhelmed her. He waited patiently for her verbal reaction.

"You wrote this?" she finally asked.

He nodded his head. She was highly impressed. He could read it from her face. Suddenly she became full of admiration for him. Her eyes said it all.

While they were still talking, a shadowy figure in a baseball cap walked past the reception into the hotel's lobby. Bimbo caught sight of him. Quickly, she stood up and offered her hand to the young man: "My name is Bimbo Johnson. It's been really nice meeting you. Do you live around this place?"

"I live just opposite this hotel".

"You come here often?"

"Yes, almost every night".

"Ok, I will see you next time, Femi. Remember your promise".

"I certainly will."

22

"I really had no option but to quit. The system was simply animalising me. It had no space for those who wanted to be original or creative". This was Femi speaking to Bimbo on why he quit his university studies. They were in Femi's room for the fourth time in two weeks. A cordial, platonic relationship had developed between them. Since her first visit, he phoned her in her office every day and she was always happy to receive his calls. They never discussed why she frequented the Ukunu Central Hotel or who the bearded man in baseball cap was.

The first time she visited him, the beauty of the disorder in his room fascinated her. Colourful posters of Malcom X, Fidel Castro, Balarabe Musa, Kwame Nkrumah, Mokwugo Okoye and Reverend Martin Luther King occupied every available space of the wall facing the door. On the wall to the right were memorable quotes. Some were cut from newspapers and magazines. She immediately fell in love with some of those quotes, which she copied out:

Failure is in a sense the highway to success, every discovery of what is false leads us to seek earnestly after what is true, and every fresh experience points to the same form of error which we shall afterwards carefully avoid. – Keats

We are living in time of great changes. The old order is crumbling fast. Our business is to seek to understand these changes and to utilise them for human progress. – Balarabe

Musa

What values can be nobler or more enduring than humility, patience, honesty and spiritual virtue? – Femi Zed

Each time she read his work, her belief that he was destined for great things was reinforced. She completely believed in his dreams and somehow lusted to be part of it. She even saw something colourful about his Spartanic lifestyle. Femi himself knew that she admired him and believed in him. He loved the fact that for once there was someone who deeply shared his conviction that he had been chosen by history and by destiny for great things. For him, that was a sign of progress. At least it helped to strengthen his belief that he was very sane, that he was not suffering from megalomania, and that his problem all along had been that people had been conspiring to prevent him from reaching his destiny. He concluded that all these were based on envy and jealousy and instantly resolved that whenever he became a great man, he would make sure that Bimbo received a good mention in his autobiography.

While Bimbo was re-reading the quotes, Femi was still busy justifying why he decided not to continue with his university studies:

"Education in this country is what I call a banking system of education. Here, the teacher knows everything while the student must accept that he or she doesn't know a thing. The teacher is the depositor, the student is the receptacle. The whole aim is to use the system of reward and punishment to eliminate those who will be very critical of the system. Do you know the whole idea behind examination and certificates?"

She folded the sheet of paper on which those quotable quotes were written and put it in her bag. She didn't quite understand a number of the words he used but she liked the seriousness on his face as he struggled pedantically to make his point. She also had a feeling that his logic was unassailable.

She shook her head in the negative.

"Well, the whole idea of examination is to test the students' willingness to conform with the system. During examinations, those who regurgitate exactly what the teachers told them will be rewarded with high marks and good certificates. On the other hand, those who question the correctness of what the teachers told them to believe as truths are failed. Take a good example. The teachers will tell you that 2 multiplied by 2 will give 4 and they expect you to memorise this answer. If you want to know why 2 multiplied by 2 should be 4 and not 15 for example, you will be failed and called a dull student. You can easily see that education in this country is not for those eager to change the way things are".

Bimbo agreed with his analysis. Her smiles and facial contours illustrated her belief in him. Her eyes reflected her sympathy with his total disgust with 'the system'.

Excited at this willing audience, Femi kept on with his analysis, his theorising, and his vision of his country. Bimbo continued to listen faithfully. But she didn't forget her appointment that evening at the Ukunu Central Hotel, suite No. 17. She was in the suite a good one-hour ahead of schedule.

23

23 October 1992 was the twentieth anniversary of the Back-to-God church. Or more precisely, it was the twentieth anniversary of the day my wife and I prayed so fervently that we got into a spiritual ecstasy and decided afterwards to give our lives to God. Our thirst for God had continued to grow, with the church blossoming. Money was steadily pouring into the church accounts. I had attained national fame as a televangelist. What else could I ask for?

One morning, I was sitting in our lounge, alone with my thoughts. It was still early in the morning, around five o'clock. Some cockerels were showing off their deep-throated crows. I heard some hens flapping their wings furiously, rebuking them to stop that nonsense. Suddenly a commotion erupted among the birds. I heard the chirruping of the young as they expressed their concerns for their safety. From the window, I saw a kite hovering menacingly at a suspiciously low altitude. There was a strong urge for me to go and scare it away. Just then I saw an embittered hen fly so high that it nearly struck the marauding kite with its poisoned beak. The kite was taken aback by this unexpected counter-attack and increased its altitude to a safer level. I gave a little smile of satisfaction and took a sip from the glass of Coca- Cola on the table.

I was reflecting. As I looked back, I felt we had come

a long way. The B-to-G church, as it was affectionately called, had grown beyond our wildest imagination. It had, within twenty years of its conception, become a household name throughout the country. It had more than two hundred local branches, and ten international branches in Ghana, Gambia and Sierra Leone.

I was very grateful to God that I had grown with the church. I had never ceased to express my gratitude to God for that: I was now known and respected within the Christian community throughout West Africa as the founder and spiritual leader of the B-to-G church. All members of the church looked up to me in the same vein as Roman Catholics looked up to the pope. Local and international branches often came on a spiritual retreat at the headquarters of the church in Lagos.

We planned to mark our twentieth anniversary with a special service. All our branches were urged to offer special prayers of thanksgiving. We encouraged as many as could afford it to come to the Lagos headquarters of the church to join in the celebration. It was going to be a very busy one for us.

In the evening, after the main celebration, my family and I decided to have a small, private commemoration. Naturally, this included prayer. This lasted for some thirty minutes. Then we settled down to eat a special dinner of Uncle Ben's rice with chicken stew. There were also some bottles of non-alcoholic wine. Bimbo was there but she didn't look especially happy. I noticed that she and my wife were avoiding eye contacts. They seemed to be nursing thinly veiled grievances against each other. I worried.

At about eleven o'clock that night, when everyone had gone to bed, I tiptoed to her room. She was still awake and seemed cross. Her face looked as if she was expecting me. I stood for a while and looked at her. She was lying face upwards on the bed. I had a strong urge to say something. My instincts warned me against it. Her eyes seemed to be accusing or blaming me for something I couldn't figure out. I fished out the note from the pocket of my pyjamas. The message was terse: *Tomorrow. Between 16.30 and 17.00 hours.*

I tiptoed out of the room without a word. From outside came the blubbering sound of an easterly October wind. Suddenly there was a power failure. From a slit in the window frame in the lounge, I could see the thick darkness outside. Lightning streaked now and again, adding a certain shadow to the stillness of the night. I entered my room and noiselessly closed the door.

The following day, Bimbo rang my wife from her office to say that one of her girlfriends was seriously ill and that she would be going to keep the friend company. She said she would spend a night with the friend. As usual my wife didn't doubt her story. She was too trusting.

Bimbo arrived at the Ukunu Central Hotel more than an hour ahead of schedule and went straight to our love nest.

24

It was around four o'clock in the afternoon. I had just finished praying. Rain had drizzled in the morning but the sun had since begun shining again. I was preparing for my appointment with Bimbo. No, my conscience was not bothering me about it. I tried not to think such thoughts any more. I couldn't see the point.

My wife burst into my room. She was looking tired and worn out. She said her illness was getting worse, that she was coughing blood. I focused my eyes on her. I remembered how she had stood by me all these years. I knew she needed me more than ever.

I had always believed that prayers could help heal the sick. But I never denied the potency of medicine. I felt that prayers alone might not be sufficient for my wife in her present condition, so I decided immediately to rush her to the General Hospital.

There was a long queue at the hospital such that it took us more than three hours to see the doctor. It took another hour to drive the less- than- a- kilometre journey to our home because of the traffic jam. By the time we got back home, it was already past nine o'clock.

I had this thing that once I gave my word for something, I was bound to keep it irrespective of changes in circumstances. For this reason, I decided that, late as it was, I must keep my date with Bimbo. Better late than never, you know.

25

After my wife had gone to bed, I called the house girl and told her that I was going to the chapel to pray, and that I might be back very late. This was not unusual, so there were absolutely no grounds for her to be suspicious.

I made sure that she saw the bible in my hand and deliberately opened a passage and began muttering some words. I heard my house-girl say something to me but pretended to be absorbed. She repeated herself, louder. I could no longer pretend not to hear her. I looked briefly in her direction and without speaking, acknowledged her greeting with a friendly nod of the head. Then I hastened towards the chapel.

I stayed in the chapel for ten minutes or so. I thought a lot about Bimbo and our appointment as I flipped through some passages of the bible. I didn't try to concentrate on God. That would be too painful. I knew that what I was doing with Bimbo was wrong but I tried not to think about it. I had convinced myself that God deliberately allowed me to play this game with Bimbo in order to use the experience to elevate me to a higher level. I also convinced myself that I could stop the game when I wanted. I always took consolation in the fact that our God was a forgiving God, that all I needed to do was go down on my knees with a broken and a contrite heart.

After being in the chapel for some ten minutes, I

sneaked out and walked some two hundred metres away from the compound. I looked from left to right to see if there was any one around who might recognise me. Then I flagged down a cab. As usual, I told the driver to stop me at a particular road junction. From there, it was a three-minute walk to where I normally hid my disguises.

I put on the baseball cap and the false beard. From there, I did the fifteen-minute walk to the Ukunu Central Hotel.

At ten o'clock I tapped gently, almost noiselessly, on the door of suite number seventeen. There was silence. Then I began hearing the deafening poundings of my heartbeat. Had Bimbo left? I tapped softly again on the door. The poundings of my heartbeat had eased. I believed she knew me well enough to know that if I didn't turn up there had to be a very important reason. I believed she regarded me as reliable.

I was caught in a web of conflicting thoughts. Should I write her a note? Should I get the key from the reception and check if she had left any message for me? Should I knock louder on the door in case she had been held captive by the god of sleep? I was still mired in these labyrinths of thoughts when, suddenly, I heard shuffling footsteps inside. The latch was lifted, and the door was pulled back.

I entered hurriedly, as I always did. The air-conditioner was humming. Bimbo was looking serious. I was pretty certain that she would understand when she heard the story. But first I had to relieve myself of these disguises. They were not exactly comfortable, you know.

I removed the baseball cap and the false beard and slumped on the bed.

"What a day!" I exclaimed, by way of an apology and

an explanation.

"You are late. You kept me waiting for so long without any consideration". She said this slowly and seriously.

"I am deeply sorry. You know I always keep to time. The fact is that just as I was preparing to come around quarter past...."

I stopped abruptly. Was I dreaming? I remained speechless. I was trembling with anger. I looked from Bimbo to the bearded young man who had just sneaked out of the suite's toilet. He looked unkempt, almost like a ruffian. He was wearing a pair of worn-out jeans, a big belt and a dirty brown shirt. He had on a red beret cap and was flying his shirt. He greeted me casually and sat on one of the chairs opposite the bed.

I looked sternly at him. If he was scared, he didn't allow it to show on his face. This infuriated me all the more. Bimbo noticed my displeasure at the presence of the young man but said nothing. Observing how surprised and dismayed I was at his presence in the suite, the young man tried to stir up a conversation.

"So you are Bimbo's maternal uncle? My name is Femi. Like Bimbo, I also come from Ibadan...."

"So what are you doing here at this time of the night? Who invited you here? Is your coming from Ibadan a passport for you to barge into this place?" I was shaking with anger as I asked these questions. The young man said nothing.

Bimbo said nothing. The air-conditioner continued to hum indifferently.

"Tell me, Bimbo, who is this young ruffian? And who brought him here? What are you two doing all alone in this room?" The young man remained unruffled. Bimbo's face showed her concern.

"Femi is not a ruffian. He is a writer. We are just

friends. There is nothing between us."

"You liar", I retorted. "You shameless prostitute. I thought you had repented your evil ways. I never expected you to stab me in the back!".

She began to cry. The young man looked concerned. My anger was choking me. The young man began to talk, calmly and confidently. The tempo of his gesticulations moved in tandem with the tenor of his voice.

"I know that as an uncle, you probably mean well in getting angry. I only plead that you make such corrections with love and not allow yourself to be overwhelmed by anger. You look like a responsible man, even a man of power. And this reminds me of the eternal words of the great Greek historian, Thucydides, when he said, and I quote: "Of all manifestations of power, restraint impresses men most."

"Shut up your dirty mouth and do not lecture me! It is people like you who make this young girl nearly incorrigible. This girl you see here is... was... a... prostitute. I have been...."

"Stop calling me a prostitute. I am... not... a prostitute. Are you a saint?" She was still crying. But a certain note of defiance had crept into her voice.

"How dare you talk to me like that, you harlot. Is this because of this stupid fellow here?".

"I don't care", she retorted stubbornly. The way she said this stabbed my ego. I immediately found myself jumping out of the bed, and slapping her. She held my shirt, meaning to fight back. The young man took sides with her and dared me to touch her again.

I suddenly realised what I was doing. I sat back on the bed. Bimbo was still holding my shirt, saying: "You must kill me today". The young man pleaded with her to let go of my shirt.

After a while, the full impact of the situation dawned

on me. I felt sorry for myself. She let go of my shirt. The young man sat down on the sofa. I began to get worried. Did he recognise me? Had Bimbo spilled the beans? If she had told him that I was just her maternal uncle, did he really believe that? Or did he think it strange that an uncle would choose a hotel suite as a meeting place with his niece? Did he know that the suite was permanently reserved for us? I began to tremble. I started to feel remorseful. A sad and nosey bile crept up my throat. I promised myself that this would be the end of my sinful relationship with Bimbo. I began to regret starting the dalliance, and playing along this far. I started feeling that what I needed urgently was to get home and pray to God – with a broken and a contrite heart.

The room was silent for some minutes after the fracas, but for the air-conditioner's monotonous groan. The young man had his head bowed. From him I looked at Bimbo. She seemed to have calmed down.

Shame seized me. Suddenly my hand touched the false beard. The baseball cap was lying beside it. I stole a quick glance at the young man. His head was still lowered to the floor. Quickly, I scooped the disguise into my bag and stood up. "Well, I am sorry for what happened. I guess I over-reacted. Goodnight to both of you". They looked at each other and said nothing.

Outside the suite, in the corridor leading to the staircase, I stopped and listened. There was no one coming or going. The light was a dim blue. I hurriedly put on the cap and the false beard, and quickened my steps to the exit.

In the cab home, my mind was not on what Bimbo and the bearded young man might be doing all alone in that suite. Rather, I was worried more about what they would be gossiping about me.

26

I felt deeply worried and ashamed of myself for many days after the incident at the Ukunu Central Hotel. How could I have descended so low? What came over me? The furious pounding of my heart hurt badly as I thought things over. At one point, I feared a heart attack. I worried that I would soon be in the throes of a scandal. The bearded young man might have recognised me. After all, who hadn't heard of the Most Reverend (Dr.) Ogwu, televangelist and founder and spiritual leader of the Back-to-God church?

I tried to convince myself that there might be a slight chance that the young man neither watched television nor interested himself in religion. At this thought, fleeting feelings of comfort flowed through my veins. But my mind suddenly shifted to a sadder terrain. I began to think about the young man and Bimbo. I wondered how close they really were and what she might told him about me.

For more than three days, I ate absolutely nothing. No, I was not fasting. I looked terrible, and lost more than seven kilos. I felt ill and emaciated.

I tried to derive strength from God, remembering His words in the Holy Book. I remembered what He said about being an absolutely forgiving God, in particular that famous phrase: *the sacrifices that are acceptable to God are a broken and a contrite heart*. I chose to do exactly that and embarked on a three-day dry fasting, from six o' clock in the morning to six in the evening. I begged God to forgive. I promised Him that if I got out of this mess, I would never allow myself to stray again.

My wife noticed my distressing condition and showed a lot of concern. She wanted to know every hour how I felt and if there was anything she could do to help. I appreciated this, though it sometimes got too much.

Many members of the church called to wish me a quick recovery. Bimbo avoided me. I also didn't particularly want to see her. But she still lived with us so I was conscious of her being around. We ran into each other on two occasions. On each occasion she missed her step and nearly fell. For my part, the illness got worse.

She got smarter in avoiding me after our second meeting. After about a week, I secretly longed to see her. I longed to see her face just to know if she felt sorry for what she did. Yes, I would also like to talk to her. Or rather, I would really like to intimidate her into telling me how much she had told her bearded young friend.

One night, I was in my room praying and feeling guilty. I was asking God never to allow this unfortunate incident to get to the ears of the rival churches. I promised God that if He helped stop this unfortunate incident from coming to light and scandalising my name, I would rededicate myself to Him and serve Him with saintly devotion and fervency.

I was deeply enmeshed in my prayers. Tears were swelling in my eyes and streaming down my cheeks. I was kneeling down in my bedroom, feeling exceptionally godly, and praying in tongues. My eyes were closed. My two hands were spread apart and held up in supplication to the Almighty God. I could sense a certain divine presence in the room and saw God in my mind's eyes washing away my sins with hyssop. I saw myself becoming whiter than snow.

Suddenly, I heard the shuffle of paper against the shiny thin carpet. I had a strong urge to open my eyes, but I resisted. I felt it could be the Holy Spirit in visible form. Was I really ready to see God? I remembered the biblical passage: *No man can see God and live.* Was I ready to die now? Well, I was in a terrible jam, but I didn't consider death a viable option.

When I opened my eyes, there was a power failure. I quickly lit a gas lamp. The rumbling sound of unfriendly thunder could be heard outside. I heard tiny footsteps walking away from my door. I took the gas lamp from where it was standing proudly on the table. I looked closer. Someone had pushed a note under the door.

I stopped my prayers and excused God. I told Him I would come back to continue the prayers, that I was just too curious. I was sure He understood. So with the gas lamp in one hand, I moved towards the door and picked up the note. My eyes ran through it greedily: She was very sorry for what happened the other night. Honestly, it wasn't her intention to embarrass me. The fact was that, after waiting so long for me, she concluded that I wouldn't turn up again. She was the one who invited that guy up that evening. No, he wasn't a ruffian – just a radical writer and a social critic. They were friends and nothing more. She could swear by the Bible or any other deity that there was nothing amorous between them. She could see that the incident had caused me a lot of emotional trauma. She was very sorry for that. She had been more troubled by the incident than me. She would wait for me between four o'clock and five o'clock tomorrow afternoon so that we could resolve the issue.

I read the note over and over again and then tore it to

shreds. I did this with all her notes. It was one way of minimizing the risk.

The following day, I had a hell of a time deciding whether I should go to meet her or not. On the one hand, I wanted very much to go in order to find out if her friend recognised me, and how much she had told him about me. On the other hand I didn't really feel like meeting her again. I was simply too ashamed of what I did that night. I felt I could understand if she had lost all respect for me.

I wasn't sure of what would be God's position on this issue, especially given the intensity of my penance, and the way I had been begging Him for forgiveness.

***

When four o'clock neared, I began pacing up and down my room. My decision up to that time was that I wouldn't go. I was still battling to convince myself that I had taken the right decision. "No, I won't go", I kept muttering to myself. Suddenly, I found myself dressing but convinced myself that it had nothing to do with the appointment. I told myself that I simply wanted to feel good. Then I had this urge to go to the town and buy some medicines. I was still feeling ill, you know.

I told my wife that I was going to buy some medicine in Lagos mainland. On the way I suddenly changed my mind. I would go and meet Bimbo. It now seemed the most appropriate thing to do. Then I remembered God and my promise to Him. A clever thought suddenly dropped into my mind- going to see Bimbo wouldn't amount to breaking my promise to Him. The decisive thing, continued this thought, was what I did with her if I met her. I smiled a half-face smile and began to explain to God that it was necessary for me to go and meet Bimbo so that I would stamp my foot on the ground and tell her straight that it was all over. I would also demand that she hand the room keys over to the hotel management. I also told God that when I got there I would use the opportunity to find out how much the bearded young man knew about me.

I got to the hotel by half past four. My eyes briefly caught the bearded young man. He had a number of books under his left armpit and was moving towards the dining room and bar. I hesitated for a while, and then quickened my steps. As I hastened towards room No.17, I wondered if he had recognised me in my disguise.

She was waiting for me. The door was slightly ajar. Inside, she was crying. I entered and shut the door.

***

"I saw your friend downstairs as I was coming up. Did you two arrange that he should come and visit you here today?" I said this even before I had fully entered the room. There was a tinge of bitterness in my voice. I was sure she sensed this. She shook her head in the negative. "Then what is he doing downstairs? I saw him moving to the bar with a bottle of Coke".

"He usually comes here. I first met him in the hotel bar. I think he lives around here. He does his writing downstairs".

"He is only a pretender. I have never heard of a writer choosing a hotel bar to do his writing. Writing is a very lonely profession and writers as a rule want to write in an atmosphere of least disturbance".

She said nothing. I took off my disguises and put them in my bag. I sat on the chair facing the bed. It was the first time I had ever sat on that chair. Her eyes showed no surprise. I contorted my face to show that I was serious about what I was doing. I was making a definitive statement that it was all over, that my visit was strictly formal and business. The game was over.

She looked away to show her displeasure in my display of excessive formality. I refused to wear a conciliatory ambience. The air conditioner in the room wasn't switched on. I didn't complain. After a long and noisy silence, I decided to break the ice.

"Does your friend know you are here?"

She shook her head in the negative. I felt calmer and more relaxed. After a while, I unconsciously looked at my watch. I had resolved that I would not spend more than fifteen minutes with her, so I decided to get straight to the point. I asked her why she wanted to see me. She said she just wanted to apologise to me so that we could continue as before. "Never", I snapped, with bitterness. I told her of my plans to terminate the tenancy of the room.

She began to sob. I remained unmoved and began to see only Satan in her. I remembered the Bible stories of how Eve led Adam astray, and how Delilah was used by Samson's enemies to get him. She blew her nose many times, probably to let me know that her crying was real. I didn't care. She stopped crying after a while, and sat up on the bed. I avoided eye contact with her.

I asked her how much her friend knew about me. Under oath, she told me that the guy certainly didn't recognise me. She also swore she told him that I was her maternal uncle, that I was always afraid that people would either poison me or set me up, and that that was why I took a permanent suite at the hotel. She said she told him that I gave her free access to the suite because she cleaned the place for me, and that she was the only one I really trusted.

I was secretly impressed with her story. I had no doubt that she was telling the truth, which made me feel more at ease. I began to glorify God in my thoughts, and to reiterate my promise never again to derail.

Another moment of noisy silence. Somewhere in the street, someone was cursing. Cries of "mobile police!" could be heard. There were more noises and what sounded like a stampede. Then silence.

I got up and said I was ready to leave. She immediately sprang on her feet and held onto my shirt. "I must go", I repeated. My voice was neither friendly nor unfriendly.

"Please. I can't do without you. I have told you that I am sorry and that it will not happen again. Please forgive me". She began to cry again. I knew I had to handle her with extra care. I also knew that her friend downstairs would immediately come to her defence if he suspected we were fighting. That would be too bad for me. Also, if I didn't play my cards right, there was the possibility of blackmail. I decided to acquire the wisdom of a serpent.

"You see, I think we need to stop seeing each other for a while until I have completely recovered. I don't have anything against you... provided you stick to our rules."

"How long will this last?"

"I don't know. Maybe a week. Maybe longer. It depends on how both of us feel about it. We will of course remain in contact through the normal channels".

She let go of her hold on my shirt. I rubbed her forehead with my hand in faked affection. She muttered something about being broke. I dipped my hand in my pocket and brought out a bundle of Naira notes. The notes were crispy, presented to the church by one of its rich members that morning as a widow's mite towards the church's evangelisation campaign.

From the bundle, I selected a few notes and squeezed them into her hand. Her face lit up, and she stroked the back of my head. I put on my disguise and left.

27

Ibegan feeling better after the meeting with Bimbo. Everyone noticed it and gave glory to God for healing me. I suspected that probably God gave my case an accelerated hearing and decided to give me another chance. Yes, Bimbo sounded very convincing: The bearded young man didn't recognise me. Bimbo didn't tell him anything incriminating.

For many hours after I got back from the hotel, I knelt in my room just laughing to myself and feeling good. My love for God had increased tenfold. My prayers to Him on this had been focused, persistent and painstaking.

I started reflecting. Maybe God wanted to use my experiences with Bimbo to teach me a lesson. I felt I had got the message. I was married and I must stick to my wife. This is what the Holy Book teaches.

The happiness on my face was contagious as I came out of my room later that evening. Three members of the church visited to see how I was doing and were all pleasantly surprised. My wife was very happy. However, the good feeling lasted for only two days.

The worries returned with a vengeance on the third day. I became sad and moody again. Bimbo! What guarantee did I have that she would not talk later? And that haggard-looking writer friend of hers! What assurance did I have they would not get more intimate, and then under the blind push of love or lust or both she would open her mouth wider than necessary?

Something suddenly hit me at the pit of my stomach. I began to feel sick. My hands were beginning to shake. Beads of sweat immediately formed on my forehead. My legs began to wobble and to sweat. I had become ill again. My bed felt too hot for comfort. I tried to pray. Images of Bimbo, in her satanic ordinariness, kept blurring the majestic picture of the Lord in my mind. I tried to sleep. It didn't work. Thoughts of Bimbo and her friend and what they were capable of doing to my reputation blocked my entrance to the leisurely world of the unconscious. In the morning, I looked worn-out and sickly. My wife became alarmed. Church members who visited our home early in the morning were urged by my wife to join her in a three-hour long prayer.

After that, I felt a little better and managed to catch some sleep. An idea suddenly dropped into my mind as I lay tossing on my bed. It unlocked the gate to the therapeutic planet of sleep, which I was only too glad to enter.

The following day, I began to work on that idea. I knew a high-ranking policeman, Okey Ezoke. We came from the same village. He was also a member of my church. I didn't think of him as being especially devoted, though he always looked pious each time he prayed. He was also a member of the group we called the financial pillars of our church. There were usually special prayers for members of this group during each service. We treated them more or less as the church's living saints. Okey Ezoke visited us every other week.

He was home. His favourite car was parked outside. I drove in and stayed with him and his wife for about thirty minutes. Then he walked me to my car. We talked about nothing in particular, just cracking jokes. Finally we hugged each other and I got into my car to leave.

I started the engine and allowed it to run for a while before I cutting it off. "Problem, Reverend?" Okey walked back towards my car.

"Not really. I just remembered something". I sensed his curiosity and chose not to start the tale. This made him even more curious. He opened the door of my car, and sat in the front seat, next to me.

It was getting darker. I couldn't really see the features of his face under the darkness. But I was pretty sure he was silently feeling impatient with me. I could imagine him restraining himself with all his effort. Normally, he didn't play games. He didn't like his time being wasted. I allowed another eternal second to pass before I began.

"Well, Okey, someone came to the church a couple of days ago and made a confession. He said he was a member of an armed gang that had been terrorising this city for so long. According to him, he has participated in at least five bank robberies within the past two months, including that robbery at Unity Bank last week where a pregnant woman was killed. You must promise never to ask me who this chap is. I believe he has repented."

He gave me his word that he would not ask for the identity of the person. Even as he said this, the curiosity in his voice was discernible.

I continued. "Well, I am telling you this because this man's colleague in crime has vowed to kill him because he said he was going straight." I paused. Okey was breathing noisily. A motorbike with a broken exhaust pipe and no headlights sped past. Okey cursed the driver under his breath. From a nearby house, a woman swore angrily at one of her eleven children, invoking the name of a local deity. From a distance the blare of disco music could be heard. I continued my story.

"My feeling is that this man has been tormented since the Unity Bank robbery but his accomplice obviously didn't want to hear anything about stopping..."

"Did the guy give you any clues about this fellow? I mean, did he give you a description of him, or tell you where he could be found?"

"Well, he did. I don't really know if I should tell you about it."

"Come on, Reverend. We are talking about someone who might kill you or me or one of our relatives. We all have an obligation to help the police."

I pretended to think about this for a while. Then I said loudly to myself: "Maybe you are right".

"Sure, I am".

"Well, the guy told me that his accomplice usually hangs out in a hotel in Ajengule. The Ukunu Central Hotel, I think. He says the guy pretends to be a writer, and that he has actually made some university students write and publish a few articles in newspapers under his name..."

Okey interrupted. "Criminals are more crafty these days. Well..." He didn't finish the second sentence he started. I didn't push him. The tone of his voice said it all. It was laden with the kind of fury we feel when mosquitoes prevent us from falling asleep with their irritating buzzes and bites.

I was about to continue my story when a nearby frog began shouting. Two other frogs quickly joined in. It seemed as if they were competing. We sat in silence, as if by some form of telepathy we had agreed to listen and play umpires. Then all of a sudden they stopped simultaneously their contest – as if they had suddenly become aware of our presence. In my mind, I declared the competition a no-contest. Okey didn't comment. We resumed our discussion.

I was the one talking: "I understand that in the day-time he works as a motor-tout. From about four to eleven in the evening, he stays at the bar of that hotel pretending to be writing one thing or another."

There was a flash of torchlight in the car. It was Okey looking at his watch. I used the opportunity to look at mine too. It was quarter past eight. "He goes to that hotel everyday?"

"That's what the guy said"

"Let me see if I can nab him there now. When I get back I will call you and tell you how it went". There was a sense of urgency in his voice. I wished him good luck and gave him God's blessing.

28

Okey called at around a quarter to eleven. He sounded very happy, self-congratulatory even. "I have sent that guy to where he rightly belongs. I think our society will be much the better without such characters". He paused. I was secretly delighted but said nothing. "The chap even tried to con me by putting on academic airs and speaking bombastic English. But I have been in this job for twenty years and I know what's what." He gave a long, throaty laugh.

"Where is the guy now?"

"In the Kirikiri maximum security prison. He's a dangerous one. If he doesn't die before his trial, he should consider himself lucky".

I asked him how long it would take to bring him to trial. He said he didn't know. Then he quickly added that it might take between two to five years. I reminded him of his promise never to ask me to disclose the identity of the guy who made the confession, and never to try to find this out on his own. He re-assured me. Finally I told him that I wouldn't like any kind of confrontation with men of the underworld, and so wouldn't like to be mentioned in connection with the arrest. Again he gave me his word.

***

The same night, I slipped in a note to Bimbo. I would

like us to meet at the usual place the following day between four o'clock and six o'clock. I knew she would be there. She had requested such a meeting a couple of days before. At that time, I had refused. I had told her I was ill.

Once in the hotel room, I got straight to the point: I had received a revelation from God. She would come into harm very soon if she remained in this city. Some people from her inglorious past were after her life. My suggestion to her as a priest, friend and father figure was to make haste and leave Lagos immediately.

I was surprised and worried that my 'vision' didn't seem to perturb her. She said that she wasn't prepared to relocate to another town. I tried to convince her but She refused to bulge. I let her know how concerned I was about her safety and promised to help her get a job if she relocated. She remained unmoved.

I felt very disappointed, and nearly lost my composure. I went home, feeling bad.

Two days after this meeting, when no one was at our home, Bimbo packed her things and left. She left no note and called no one. My wife was worried, and called her office but was told that Bimbo no longer worked there. No, they didn't know anything about her whereabouts. No, they didn't know if she had found another job. No, she wasn't fired, she just stopped turning up.

I called the Ukunu Central Hotel from a public telephone and asked about the lady who normally stayed in room No.17. They told me that she had not been seen for about a week. I suspected that she had taken my advice after all.

29

Bimbo wasn't completely taken by surprise. She had always known it would happen one day. It had been the pattern in her life. Every good thing she stumbled upon had a way of slipping through her fingers.

Her life had been stable for some time now. She didn't believe she would ever move on after the departure of Helle, but she now considered herself a relatively happy person. She attributed this to the two most important individuals in her life- her radical writer friend, and myself.

Now, she had lost my support. Actually, she felt that she lost me on that first day we did it. She had silently predicted that our relationship would only come to an unhappy conclusion. And she had been on her guard for signs of that inevitable dénouement.

She swore that she would never allow her relationship with Femi to be tainted in the way she allowed ours to be defiled. She liked Femi. His type was few and far between. He talked nicely to her, listened compassionately to her, and never demanded sex. She only wished that I could understand that the guy had no amorous interest in her, that he was simply a sweet person.

She decided to go and see him at the Ukunu Central Hotel. He wasn't there. She bought a bottle of Coke and chose to while away time at the bar, hoping that he might turn up later. He didn't. It was the first time since she knew him that he had failed to appear. When he still didn't show up by nine o'clock, she became alarmed. She feared that he had fallen sick.

She knew where he lived. She had been there a couple of times but didn't really like visiting him at home. Not that she was afraid but just that she felt her presence there always made him conscious of the frugality of the room.

At around ten o'clock, she found herself knocking on his door. He wasn't home.

The following evening she returned to the hotel. Again he didn't show up. She went again to where he lived. The door to his room was firmly locked. She returned again to the hotel the following evening but yet again he failed to appear. After a while she decided to ask one of the hotel receptionists.

The man she asked was the same old man who believed that the bearded young man was another Chinua Achebe or Wole Soyinka in the making. He was full of sadness as he narrated the story: "Two days ago, two policemen came here and arrested him. They accused him of being an armed robber and handcuffed and manhandled him. Miss, the guy is a genius in the making. I am almost seventy years old. I can recognise a bad character when I see one. That guy isn't one. I think someone framed him. I understand they have put him in the Kirikiri without a trial. Miss, I weep for this country."

Bimbo was overwhelmed and stood fixated. She had lost all sense of feeling. The old man at the reception was angrily hitting his hand against the desk in front of him. He was bitterly murmuring something about the country being rotten to the core. A short bald man in his sixties was shuffling down from one of the chalets upstairs, his right hand inside the trousers of a teenage girl. He was giggling loudly and boasting about the number of containers he owned on the wharf. The girl was leaning drunkenly on him, swinging her hips obscenely each time the bald man went from her trousers to her underwear. She was emptying his pockets with her right hand. Across the street, two young men suddenly started fighting. One was cursing and boasting that he was a cousin of the president. The other broke an empty bottle of beer on his head and dared him to tell his cousin, the president.

Bimbo recollected herself and became acutely aware of what she had just heard.

She recognised that the first thing to do was to calm her nerves and think rationally. She had heard from one of her teachers that decisions taken emotionally were often laden with bad judgement. How could she bring herself to think rationally under the current circumstances?

She ordered a bottle of Coke. For two long hours, she sat in the hotel's bar, thinking, and occasionally sipping the drink. She was now beginning to think in a more detached manner. She concluded that Femi had been set up. She also felt that she knew the perpetrator and the motive. Bimbo had never felt so embittered. It was then that she took the decision to leave. She also resolved that she must fight to convince everyone that Femi was innocent.

The following day, when everyone had gone out of the home, she packed her belongings and, without leaving a message, departed our house.

30

One of Bimbo's girlfriends lived alone in a room in Ikeja, one of the better suburbs in Lagos. She shared a kitchen and a toilet with twenty-two other tenants in the compound. This was to be Bimbo's new abode.

The first evening, as they sat gossiping under the semi-darkness of candles, a pot-belied man in a flowing *agbada* walked in. Bimbo knew he was coming. She had in fact met the man a couple of times before. He was her friend's employer and sugar daddy, and Bimbo had always thought him amiable.

That evening, the sugar daddy ate dinner with them. They shared jokes and gossiped. One discussion led to another, and Bimbo was offered a job. She started the following morning.

***

A new home and a new job weren't enough to make her forget. She was still deeply embittered. How could someone who called himself a man of God descend to such a gutter level? She had always been distrustful of people who hawked their piety. She remembered her experiences with members of her school's SU and sighed. Then she recalled how I had played the good father- figure and wise counsellor to her in the begin-ning, only to bring out my fangs at the slightest oppor-tunity. As she reflected over these on her way to the

Kirikiri prison that Saturday morning, she began to see the hidden wisdom in her friend's advice that she should stay out of my sight. I could do anything to silence her.

***

Femi had not the slightest idea why he was brought to Kirikiri. He had concluded that it was a case of mistaken identity but had tried not to argue when the Police handcuffed him. The only thing he asked was what his offence was but the answer he got was a deafening slap from one of the officers. He had heard another officer say something like, "Nemesis has caught up with you. For too long you and your partners in crime have been terrorising this city."

He followed his instincts and submitted himself to arrest and humiliation. He knew that if he tried to prove his innocence there, he would most likely be shot dead and the shooter would very easily get away with it. As his mind wandered, he could hear the police offering explanations for his death:

In the late hours of yesterday, the leader of the most notorious criminal gang in this city was shot dead while exchanging fire with two policemen. The police had acted on a tip-off and had gallantly burst into the criminals' hideout. Two other members of the gang escaped with serious gunshots but the police succeeded in seizing their ammunitions.

Innocent inhabitants of Lagos can now breathe a sigh of relief. Last night, at around ten o'clock, the most wanted criminal in the city was gunned down by the police while violently resisting arrest.

It always pays to co-operate with the police. Yesterday night, a young man suspected of being behind most of the bank robberies and ritual murders in this city was killed by an accidental discharge from the gun of a police officer. He was shot dead while trying to disarm a police officer that had come to arrest him.

He wished to exercise the option of remaining silent but of the policemen smacked him roughly on the face for his refusal to talk, despite being cautioned that anything he said would be used against him in a court of law. He was confused. The beating and kicking continued. He felt the pain but refused to cry. His tormentors got even more furious and claimed that his refusal to cry was a clear evidence that he was a hardened criminal. One of them suddenly hit him across the left ear. The pain was excruciating and he gave out an agonising groan. One of the four officers accused him of pretending to feel the pain. Another asked him in a calm whisper if he was ready to cut a deal with them.

The interrogation was a formality. Police Superintendent Okey Ezoke had given instructions that Femi should be thrown straight into jail and that there should be no hurry to bring him to trial. His reason? The tip-off had come from a most impeccable source.

31

Femi felt the disquieting warmth of the sun and the sadness of the birds' songs as he walked to the dining hall. For a moment he forgot himself and his condition and began to wonder if Mother Nature was equally fair to all her children. Were the people in the tropics particularly cursed? Why is it so hot down here? Why was it that most parts of Africa are given less than four months of rainfall in a year? Why is it that most of the reptiles found in his part of the world are more dangerous than those in the Western world? He remembered the case of mosquitoes and attempted a smile. One of his former lecturers, a Scandinavian, had told him that there were also mosquitoes in western countries, and that they also bite. But he also told them that, unlike in Africa, those mosquitoes don't carry the parasites that spread malaria. If this was true, then why the discrimination? Then he remembered the photograph that Madam Cash had taken during one of her trips to London. There were pigeons literally perching on her head. The thought of this swelled his face with suppressed fury. He knew that birds in his country did not allow such familiarity. He sighed loudly. As he did so, a lush of westerly wind caressed his cheek. He felt a therapeutic coolness, through a miasma of veins down to his bare feet. Suddenly he became conscious of someone behind him.

Femi was walking slightly ahead of him. He was not

an inmate or a prison guard. He wore an ill-fitting black coat and red trousers and had the exaggerated swagger of self-importance. Femi turned and looked straight at him. Though the man was wearing dark glasses, Femi felt he saw in his eyes a desire to talk. The prison warder shepherding them to lunch moved to jump on him. The man in the red trousers nodded to him that it was all right. The prison warder saluted and ran after the others, shouting, "Hey you there, stop falling out of the line or I will deal with you ruthlessly".

Femi stepped aside. The man gave him a half smile and licked his lips. Some weaverbirds were singing nonchalantly. The prison warder farted loudly. The prisoners covered their noses and laughed noisily and derisively.

The man in the red trousers led Femi to one of the complex's numerous narrow offices.

It didn't take him long to recognise the man. The horizontal marks on each cheek were unmistakable. He was one of the officers who had interrogated him when he was first brought to Kirikiri. Suddenly, a pang of fear stabbed him at the pit of his stomach. Had the man come to take him away for execution? Was this how he would meet his end?

They sat in the stuffy office, with Femi visibly trembling. The man was calm, in a way that heightened Femi's anxiety. Femi didn't like this psychological terrorism. Why was it taking him so long to explain his purpose?

Seemingly reading his mind, he began to talk. He wasn't barking out orders or threats. He looked straight and steadily into Femi's eyes and talked in a fatherly manner. He asked: "You do recognise me, don't you?" Femi nodded his head. He recalled that the man didn't contribute much when the other police officers were interrogating and threatening him.

The man allowed a long minute of silence to over-shadow them. He tapped his cheap ballpoint pen on the hard and swarthy table. Femi's mind was racing through a labyrinth of depressing thoughts. Outside, the sun intensified its heat. The policeman wiped away beads of sweat on his forehead and used the same handkerchief to absorb the dampness of his armpits. He switched on the standing electric fan. There was no power. He smiled and Femi noticed for the first time beads of sweat hanging from his massive moustache. "Why did you refuse to talk when we were interrogating you?"

Silence. Silent transmission of riotous thoughts. Femi shifted in his seat. For a moment the thought that the whole situation might be working towards his inevitable greatness hovered in his mind. He quickly brushed it aside with a repressed sigh. He wasn't sure if he really wanted to be a great man. If only he had finished his university education!

A large and lively picture of Madam Cash suddenly stood clear and pretty in his mind. He swallowed hard, his eyes reddening. His right toe began to twitch. The thought of God entered his mind and briefly soothed his troubled soul. The man continued to gaze at him. Femi carefully avoided his eyes.

The man broke his train of thought: "Tell me, and I really want you to tell me the whole truth, did you commit the crimes?" His voice was calm, non-judgmental, and even a little friendly.

Femi shook his head. The man tapped his pen on the table. At the same time, he sized up Femi, looking for subtler ways of getting to the truth. "Have you ever committed a crime? Another shake of the head in the negative.

The man became silent again. A big rat ran out of a hole in the wall. It sat courageously and looked condescendingly from Femi to the policeman. As the man resumed talking, the rat dashed back through the hole from where it came, as if daring them to catch it.

"Why do you think you were arrested?

"I have no idea."

"Someone gave us the tip-off that led to your arrest. He is a man of God and everyone respects him. Why do you think he should give us that information if you were innocent?"

"I don't know".

The man intensified his piercing gaze. Femi respectfully avoided his eyes. Power suddenly came on. The man eagerly put on the cranky electric fan. It blew heavy particles of dirty brown dust on Femi's white uniform. The man pressed a knob on the fan and it stopped rotating, blowing only in the direction he was sitting. The handkerchief on the table was tossed into the air and rested on the man's head. He removed it perfunctorily and put it in his left trouser pocket.

"What do you do for a living?" The question came like a bombshell.

"Well, I am a writer. I have worked for the Sunday Times".

"Can anyone in the Sunday Times identify you, and vouch for your integrity? Do you have any record of your publications?"

"Yes. The editor of the Sunday Times knows me. I have copies of my publications in my room. I live at No.9 Ozubulu Street, Ajegunle".

The man took notes of this information on a piece of paper. He got up, smiled from the corner of his mouth, and left.

32

Outside, the sun blazed with alacrity. The man who had just spoken to Femi still believed his intuition that Femi was an innocent man. He was suspicious of the haste with which Okey Ezoke had assumed the young man was guilty. He suspected that something was amiss.

No, this had nothing to do with his rivalry with Okey Ezoke. He was merely being a conscientious policeman. He swore that he would get to the bottom of the case. He would go straight to the young man's home, and from there he would go and talk to the editor of the Sunday Times.

He had just come outside the Kirikiri complex when a young lady approached him and politely asked, "Sir, how does one visit a prison inmate?"

He gave her directions to the compound. The lady thanked him and quickened her step.

Unconsciously he asked: "Whom do you want to see?"

The lady turned, hesitated for a moment, and replied: "Femi. Femi Zed". The policeman smiled and moved closer to her. For more than ten minutes they stood talking. Yes, she knew the prisoner. No, he was not her boyfriend, just a good friend. No, he would never do such a thing; he was just a poor idealist. Yes, she had read some of his stuff. Yes, someone framed him and she knew the person and the motive.

Bimbo began an angry narration of the incident that took place at the hotel. The policeman could hardly restrain his enthusiasm. He convinced Bimbo to follow him to the young man's home.

That evening, the policeman invited Roy Akpu, editor of the sensational Newskick magazine, for a bottle of beer.

Roy Akpu was taken aback when he heard the story. He said he had met the young man a couple of times, and that though he disagreed with his brand of radicalism, he could vouch for his integrity. He swore to get to the heart of the matter.

The following morning, the office of the weekly Newskick magazine was awash with activity. There was a sense of urgency among the journalists. A major scoop was imminent. Roy had assembled a formidable team to handle the assignment, with three freelancers especially hired to join the team working on the story. Roy chose to head the team of investigators himself. This was a rarity, and heightened the sense of urgency surrounding the case. They had a week to complete the assignment.

33

It was Sunday. I had just finished the Sunday service, and was in my room trying hard to relax. In two hours' time, my TV programme, Family Life, would be aired.

Suddenly, I heard a woman's voice: "This is blackmail! This is blackmail! This is the work of the devil! You evil powers in high places, you dark principalities, you must never prevail over God's children, for He that is in us is much greater than he that is in you." Several angry voices soon joined in the condemnation of the supposed blackmail.

From my room, I heard the angry babble of terribly disappointed voices in the lounge. I got out of the bed and began moving towards the direction of the upset voices.

Six heads were grouped together. I moved closer to see the object of attraction. It was the latest edition of the Newskick.

The woman holding the magazine respectfully handed it over to me. There were tears in her eyes. My wife was sobbing. She looked at me as I read the magazine. Her eyes were both sympathetic and accusatory. There were similar looks on the faces of the others. A tiny voice said, "This is sheer wickedness, a pure vendetta. This is a calculated campaign of calumny."

The headline was in bold red: *DECEIVING IN THE NAME OF GOD: Reverend Ogwu in love scandal.* The caption was written above a photograph of me. My hands immediately began to shake, and quickly became damp. My legs began to wobble.

A member of the Newskick staff had approached me shortly after the magazine came to hear my own side of the story and had demanded a huge sum of money to 'kill' the story. I had initially refused, swearing to him that I was innocent of the accusations. The following day, however, I called him to offer the money. I explained that I was paying the money only because I didn't want a scandal to ruin the good name of the Back-to-God church. He accepted the money and swore to me that the story would never see the light of the day. When the story did not appear on the weekly magazine two weeks after this transaction, I concluded that the man had kept his part of the bargain.

With a shaking hand, I flipped through the pages to where the cover story began. The picture of me on this page was larger than the one on the cover page. It was an artist's impression. I was portrayed in pensive mood, with my head resting thoughtfully on my right hand.

I began to run my eyes through the piece. It was about my life, from the time I was born to the time I became a politician, to the foundation of the Back-to-God church, and to Bimbo coming to live with us. There was another piece in a box about the Ukunu Central Hotel. The story detailed how I kept a suite under a false name, and how I visited there in disguise.

With a pounding heart and trembling hands, I turned over the page. There was an imposing photograph of Bimbo. The story was about her birth at Ibadan to a mad woman known as Tokunbo. I stopped as I read this. I couldn't take any more. My underpants became hot and wet. Tears overwhelmed my eyes. I was shaking compulsively. Someone put her hand on my shoulder and began to cry. I looked at my wife. She too was crying. I tried to buckle up courage and read on. The paper nearly fell from my hands. I tightened my grip and forced myself to focus on the page.

There was a photograph of a young bearded man, and a fat, happy-looking woman with grey hair. I felt I had seen the face of the bearded young man before. I looked closely at the name of the fat woman. The magazine called her Madam Cash.

Femi was adopted just before the civil war began. He was born to Ibo parents, who had fled for their life, leaving the child and their nanny, Lucy, behind. It was from Lucy that Madam Cash adopted the child.

Newskick investigations revealed that when the Most (Reverend) Ogwu fled Ibadan, he left without one of his sons, Obi, and his house-help, Lucy. Is Femi Zed actually Obi Ogwu? If so, has the Most Reverend Ogwu been behind the unjust imprisonment of his own son because of a lady young enough to be his grand daughter?

I stopped reading. I could no longer see anything as I gazed on the words in the magazine. Something was vibrating in my head. A feeling of nausea overwhelmed me. I heard my wife asking painfully if I was all right. Another person recited Psalm 23. I tried to smile, but failed. Unconsciously, I turned again to the page about Bimbo. I flipped through the pages to the stuff about Tokunbo. I tried to laugh.

Suddenly the open jaws of a crocodile rushed towards me. I tried to run. My legs were paralysed. I tried to fight with my arms. It numbed my hands with an emission of rays. Then it rushed towards me, swallowing me inside its silent black belly.

I awoke two days later in a hospital bed.

Ordering this book

Broken Dreams is published in both print and electronic (ebook) formats.

The print version could be bought from most reputable booksellers around the world. In the UK, the major distributors of the print version include:
• Amazon.co.uk,
• Lightning Source UK.
• Gardners
• Bertrams
• Chypher

In the US, the major distributors of the print version include:
• Amazon.com
• Lightning Source Inc.
• Ingram, Baker & Taylor,
• NACSCORP,
• Matthews Medical

Distributors of the electronic (ebook) version include:
• Amazon.com
• Amazon.co.uk
• Amazon.de
• Amazon.jp
• Powell.com
• Booksite.com
• Adamant Media

Please direct enquiries to any of the above distributors or contact us directly at:
Adonis & Abbey Publishers Ltd
P.O. Box 43418
London
SE11 4XZ
Phone: 020 77938893

Or visit our website at: http\\:www.Adonis-abbey.com